"You're having my baby." He didn't say it as a question, even though his mind was spinning with them.

Jade nodded. "Very good. Yes, I am."

"What are we going to do?"

She straightened, coolness chilling her eyes. "*You're* not going to do anything. *I'm* going to have a baby in January." She must have seen the confusion in his eyes. "What I'm saying is you're off the hook. I don't need or expect your help with anything. I'll raise her myself."

"The hell you will." Trent ground the words out through his clenched teeth. "If it's my child—wait. Did you say *her*?" A baby girl. Visions of pink satin and lace filled his head. He was going to be the father of a little girl. Maybe.

Jade's eyes narrowed on him. "Well, that was fast. You went from not believing me to threatening me."

"I didn't threaten you. But if this *is* my child, then I'm sure as hell going to be involved in raising her." He paused. "You know for sure it's a girl?"

She nodded, her eyes still guarded. "It's a girl. How exactly do you think you're going to be..." she made air quotes with her fingers "...*involved in raising her*? You live in Denver. I live in Gallant Lake. You're a sperm donor, Trent, not a father."

Dear Reader,

This is my seventeenth romance with Harlequin, and book seven of my Gallant Lake Stories series. But it's my very first surprise baby romance! The trope is *so* popular with romance readers, and I was honestly nervous about doing it justice.

I ended up having so much fun with this holiday story. Twice-divorced Trent has major trust issues, particularly after his last ex shook his self-confidence to the core. He doesn't trust his own judgment—he can't help wondering if this baby is really his. But he has no doubts about his growing feelings toward Jade.

When Jade opens a Greek bakery in Gallant Lake, she never planned on doing it while pregnant after a passionate no-names-exchanged one-night stand months earlier. Then the guy shows up at her bakery, staring at her baby bump, full of questions. Sure, she *can* do this alone, but the more time she spends with Trent, the more she realizes she doesn't want to. The one place in her life where she feels she truly belongs is in Trent's arms. But she needs to know he's all in before they can truly become a family.

No book happens in a vacuum. A sincere thank-you to my readers, and to my supportive family and friends. Thank you also to my wonderful Harlequin editor, Gail Chasan, and to my agent, Jill Marsal. And most of all, thanks to my husband—I *always* know I belong in his arms.

Jo McNally

Expecting His
Holiday Surprise

———

JO McNALLY

HARLEQUIN
SPECIAL
EDITION

Recycling programs
for this product may
not exist in your area.

ISBN-13: 978-1-335-72435-9

Expecting His Holiday Surprise

Copyright © 2022 by Jo McNally

Harlequin Enterprises ULC
22 Adelaide St. West, 41st Floor
Toronto, Ontario M5H 4E3, Canada
www.Harlequin.com

Printed in U.S.A.

Jo McNally lives in upstate New York with one hundred pounds of dog and two hundred pounds of husband—her slice of the bed is very small. When she's not writing or reading romance novels (or clinging to the edge of the bed), she can often be found on the back porch sipping wine with friends while listening to great music. If the weather is absolutely perfect, Jo might join her husband on the golf course, where she tends to feel far more competitive than her actual skill level would suggest.

You can follow Jo pretty much anywhere on social media—and she'd love it if you did—but you can start at her website, jomcnallyromance.com.

Books by Jo McNally

Harlequin Special Edition

Gallant Lake Stories

A Man You Can Trust
It Started at Christmas...
Her Homecoming Wish
Changing His Plans
Her Mountainside Haven
Second-Chance Summer

HQN

Rendezvous Falls

Slow Dancing at Sunrise
Stealing Kisses in the Snow
Sweet Nothings by Moonlight
Barefoot on a Starlit Night
Love Blooms
When Sparks Fly

Visit the Author Profile page at Harlequin.com for more titles.

This book is dedicated to romance readers everywhere, who love their tropes and demand their happily-ever-afters. In a stress-filled world, we want to dive into a story and be secure in the knowledge that love will win. It's our daily dose of hope.

Thank you for choosing to read my HEAs!

Chapter One

Late April...

Jade Malone didn't normally drink blue alcohol.
She preferred her vodka on ice and crystal clear,
thank you very much. But as she walked into the
ballroom of the Gallant Lake Resort for her half sister's wedding reception, the champagne flutes were
filled with bright blue liquid.

But hey, it was alcohol, so she gave it a go...and
nearly spit the blue stuff on the poor, white-jacketed
server holding the tray.

"What on *earth*...?"

The server's mouth twitched sympathetically.
"The bride told us to call it 'Sapphire Seduction,'
ma'am."

There was a gravelly chuckle behind her as the server moved away. "Seduction is an odd word to use for a wedding cocktail, don't you think? I mean, she's already seduced him, right? Isn't that why we're here?"

Jade looked over her shoulder at the stranger, who smiled and lifted a tumbler of amber liquid in a mock toast before he spoke again. "I take my seduction exclusively from a whiskey bottle."

He was a good-looking guy, but not in a pretty, Hollywood sort of way—despite the dark blond hair that fell across his forehead. His face was all sharp angles, with craggy lines around his eyes, as if he'd spent a lot of time outdoors. His build was tall and lean. Jade was six feet tall herself, *without* the expensive three-inch heels she wore. She refused to slump around in flats just to avoid intimidating shorter men. Also, it annoyed her stepmother when Jade towered over her. She found herself looking straight into this man's eyes, which were the same color as the whiskey he was drinking. He nodded toward the glass in her hand. "I took a sip earlier, and I'm pretty sure the bride hijacked a cocktail normally known as a Deep Blue Sea—vodka, bitters and blue curacao."

That was such a typical Ashley move, to take something someone else had and claim it as her own. Including Ashley's new husband, who used to be engaged to Ashley's former best friend.

She drained her glass—only because it was right there in her hand—and watched the stranger's mouth slowly curve into a smile. Whiskey Guy had a great smile—confident, amused, with just a hint of sensuality. She'd bet that when he wanted to turn it up, he could melt hearts with that heat. Not to mention melting panties.

He gestured toward the blue satin gown that swept around her ankles. "At least it matches your dress."

She tipped the empty glass in his direction. "It definitely matches my mood."

He arched one brow. "Sweet, but dangerous?"

"More like nobody here wants it, but it's doing its job, anyway."

He nodded sympathetically. "I get it. I'm here under duress myself. I don't even know the happy couple."

She wasn't sure if he was referring to Ashley's parents or Kyle's. She also wasn't sure why he'd be at a wedding if he didn't know the bridal couple.

"I'm family," she pointed out, as much to herself as to him, "but sometimes I barely know them either." A waiter walked by with a tray of blue cocktails. She grabbed one and took a sip. The taste was growing on her, as was the burn that followed.

Whiskey Guy studied her for a moment, and she wondered if he might be just the thing to help make this evening bearable. If only her stepmom hadn't invited Jade's *ex* to "complete the party" at her table, this guy could be the one to complete her party, instead.

"I don't get it." He looked around the room. "It's a bunch of strangers all dressed up and pretending to be happy for people they probably couldn't pick out of a lineup if they weren't wearing the obvious costumes. Are Kyle and Ashley gonna be happy? Who the hell knows?" He shook his head. "This one night isn't going to make or break them, either way. But everyone acts like the wedding day is the ultimate relationship launcher."

"Relationship launcher? I like that." Jade grinned. "Weapons-grade romance."

This guy was even more cynical about weddings than she was. The ballroom was beginning to fill with people. She could easily vanish after the cake was cut, and no one would notice. Except perhaps her stepmother, Marla Malone, who was headed her way right that moment, marching across the ballroom with Jade's father in tow.

Here we go. Whiskey Guy would have to remain an enigma.

She flashed him a quick smile and set her glass on a table. "Duty calls. Excuse me."

As she walked away, he called after her. "Maybe I'll see you for a dance later?"

She looked over her shoulder. "A dance? Aren't you afraid of friendly fire?"

He didn't answer, just lifted his glass in another toast before draining it. The casual conversation with a total stranger had helped calm her nerves. She felt more grounded as she greeted her father and step-mother with quick air kisses. Dad looked great in his tux. His reddish-brown hair was just beginning to show some gray around his temples, and it made him look more handsome than ever. He held Jade's hands for an extra moment, giving them a sympathetic squeeze. Ashley's elaborate wedding preparations had taken a toll on all of them, and Marla had been a textbook Monster of the Bride.

Marla had been nice enough when she'd married Phil Malone. Jade was ten at the time, still grieving her mother's death and coping with the move from Chicago to St. Louis. Jade felt like an outsider, with her dark Mediterranean complexion compared to Marla's bright blond hair and alabaster skin. Golden-haired Ashley was born two years later. As the girls grew up, Marla made it very clear where her love and loyalty resided. And it wasn't with her tall, athletic, outspoken stepdaughter.

"There you are, darling!" Marla looked her up and down like she was looking for something to criticize. "You disappeared so quickly from the photo shoot that I thought perhaps you were ill. And yet, here you are, perfectly fine."

"The photographer said he was finished with the

family photos, Marla. So I left. It's not like I was in the bridal party." Even though the bride was her half sister, she hadn't been asked. With a twelve-year age difference, they'd never been very close. "I'm sure Ashley won't miss me."

Marla glanced around furtively. "Don't use my first name. I told you, tonight I'm Mom."

Jade started to say something sarcastic, but her father's warning look made her press her lips together in silence. He loved his wife. Despite the constant microaggressions Marla either knowingly or subconsciously aimed her way, Jade had to admit that the woman seemed to genuinely care for her father.

"Sure... *Mom*. Excuse me, but I think I'll get another of those delicious blue drinks." She leaned forward and gave a conspiratorial wink. "Such a clever idea to have the drinks match the bridal party." And Jade, but only because Marla had insisted she wear blue to "blend in" in the family photos. Translation: buy your own dress, but make sure it's still an unflattering shade of turquoise.

Marla preened at the compliment. "Wasn't it, though? You know how much your sister adores blue!" Right now *everyone* knew how much Ashley liked blue, since every conceivable surface was bathed in the color. "You and Brant make such a stunning couple, sweetie. Both so...statuesque." Brant was six-nine. He was also a jerk. Jade barely kept herself from rolling her eyes. Marla had an odd obsession with pointing out how tall Jade was. Even now, she pursed her lips and looked down at the stilettos Jade wore. "Were those heels really necessary?"

"Brant and I are *not* a couple," Jade replied as civilly as possible. "And thanks for noticing my new shoes. They're my favorite part of the outfit."

Marla ignored the subtext. "We needed a plus-one for you, to balance the family table. It's just one night—it won't kill you to smile and have a little fun together. Who knows? Maybe you'll reconnect. After all, love is in the air tonight!" Marla turned to her husband. "Speaking of which, we need to get the happy bride and groom in here and on their thrones."

Unfortunately, Marla wasn't exaggerating. They'd actually brought in *thrones* for Kyle and Ashley to sit on at the head table. Jade's dad took her hand and tugged her close for a quick hug, whispering in her ear as he did.

"Try to enjoy yourself, Jadie, and stow that sharp tongue of yours. After tonight, we can all get back to our normal lives." She nodded and gave him a quick peck on the cheek to let him know she'd do her part. Dad was right—just a few more hours to go. The only problem? Getting back to *normal life* wasn't all that appealing either.

Normal life meant job hunting in St. Louis while struggling to hang on to her downtown apartment.

After the five-star restaurant where she'd been pastry chef was sold and converted to a sports bar four months ago, she'd been forced to burn through a chunk of the small inheritance she'd received from her grandmother. She'd been saving that money to open her own bakery someday. Dad kept telling her she could move back into her old room at the house, but that thought made her toes curl inside these designer slingbacks she'd splurged on for this damn wedding—right before losing her job. She headed for her table. One problem at a time.

Dinner was an adventure in avoiding Brant's grabby hands and his annoying comments about how *exotic* she looked. God, she hated that word. Brant and Jade had been together for a nanosecond two years ago. But he was a friend of the groom, and *tall*, so naturally Marla decided they were perfect. There was nothing *perfect* about the way Brant's hand kept drifting to her thigh, or the comments he made under his breath. He thought it was hot that she still had "muscles instead of curves." He was up for a "walk down memory lane" with her tonight, if she was willing.

She wasn't willing. Not even close.

She held it together long enough to watch the happy couple cut the seven-tiered cake and do a choreographed dance to an Ed Sheeran song that Ashley was hoping would go viral. By the time the dance party really started to get rolling, Jade was done. Done smiling so everyone would think she was an adoring big sister. Done laughing at the unfunny and borderline offensive jokes Brant kept telling. Just…done.

She was headed for the French doors leading to the veranda when Ashley caught her by the arm and held on with a surprisingly aggressive grip.

"Oh no, you don't! You can't leave yet." Ashley was smiling, but there was a hint of desperation to it. "Brant looks like a lost puppy over there. Besides, the videographer wants to see us all dancing to that Bruno Mars song. He's going to make a montage, and he thinks it will get a ton of views."

Ashley had a paltry few thousand followers on Insta, but insisted on telling everyone she was a "lifestyle influencer." Jade had warned her more than once that she was going to end up breaking her neck in some stupid selfie photo stunt gone wrong.

The happy couple discovered not enough people were willing to fly to some exotic locale for a trendy *destination* wedding, which was why they'd ended up in the Catskills, near where the groom had grown up. Marla had been in a snit about it at first, until she read some article that called the upscale Gallant Lake Resort a "well-kept secret" for elegant weddings, and that some famous people had been married here. Jade had to admit the place was beautiful.

The resort was elegant, but the town itself was low-key and relaxing, all nestled on a pretty lake surrounded by mountains.

"Jade? You can't go yet." Ashley still wore her steely smile.

Jade had six inches on her half sister, so it didn't take a lot of effort to pull away from her grip. "I just need some fresh air." And a whole lot of space between herself and her family. She took a steadying breath. "Ashley, today is supposed to be about starting a new life with the man you love, not getting likes from random strangers online."

Ashley's lower lip extended in a pout. That had stopped being cute when she was eight. "Come *on*, Jade. One more dance. Please?"

Jade relented, and regretted it instantly. While she had been sipping soda water in between blue cocktails in an attempt to keep her wits, Brant had been doing the opposite. He was weaving dangerously and leaned on Jade as they danced. He trod on her feet and mumbled something that sounded like an apology before doing it again. Then his hand dropped down and cupped her butt, squeezing so tightly Jade let out a curse. He repeated the move, then brushed his wet lips along her neck in some sort of drunken kiss move.

Okay, that's it, that's the line.

She shoved hard at Brant's shoulders, sending him

staggering backward on the dance floor. He bumped into Ashley and Kyle. The groom stepped on the edge of Ashley's gown as he tried to keep his balance, causing it to tear under her arm. Ashley called her new husband a very bad word. Loudly. And all of it played out in front of the videographer. Who also caught the moment when Brant went careening into a waiter and his tray, sending champagne flutes of Sapphire Seduction all over a table of senior citizens. By the time someone caught Brant and held him still and upright—was that *Whiskey Man?*—the room had erupted in chaos. People were holding their phones up to record the moment. Ashley was sobbing. Marla was fuming.

A horrified laugh started to well up in Jade's chest. It would be wrong to laugh. Very wrong. She bit her lip. And still the laughter bubbled up. She needed to get out of there. But she wasn't fast enough to escape Marla, who blocked her just as she reached the doors to the veranda.

"I can't believe you're laughing right now." Marla's whisper was harsh. "You've always been so jealous of Ashley."

Jade's jaw dropped. "Excuse me?"

"Why else would you work so hard to ruin this day?"

She may not be fond of Marla, but it still stung to hear the woman who'd essentially raised her suggest that she would *intentionally* try to ruin her sister's happiness. Her stepmom really did see her as a stain on their otherwise perfect family aesthetic.

When she turned away from Marla's judgmental glare, she saw her father comforting Ashley near the dance floor. You could tell right away they were father and daughter. Both with light hair and fair skin, her head on his shoulder. If Marla's words were a knife in her gut, seeing them together like that was the final twist. Jade plastered on a bland expression, then turned back to Marla, gesturing at the guests who were still holding up their phones. "I don't know why you're upset. Ashley wanted to go viral, and now she definitely will. It's probably already up on Fail. com. You're welcome."

Shouldering her way past her sputtering stepmother, Jade headed out to the veranda. Her chest felt like it was caught in a vise. She bit the inside of her lip to keep from crying. She needed to put some distance between herself and the wreck of a reception.

If she could have skipped this expensive and angst-filled trip to Gallant Lake, she would have. She was unemployed and could feel her dream of opening her own pastry shop in downtown St. Louis slipping away. She'd been just about ready to swallow her pride and ask her father for a loan. After tonight's fiasco, that option was probably off the table for a while.

Outside, the veranda was packed with people, some of them now dancing to the music which had restarted inside. Strings of tiny lights sparkled from a vine-tangled arbor overhead. Jade paused just long enough to look back through the windows. It was the father/daughter dance. Her dad was swaying comfortably along with Ashley in the center of the floor, smiling down at her proudly.

She headed to the veranda bar for another drink. The bartender was busy chatting with a woman at the opposite end of the bar, so Jade reached over and grabbed an open bottle of wine, intending to fill her own glass. Then she decided *what the hell*, and just took the bottle, leaving her glass behind her as she walked out onto the lawn alone. Tears were already threatening to make a mess of her makeup. Jade *hated* tears.

Head held high, jaw clenched, she marched down the manicured lawn. The lakeshore was quiet and there was no one else in sight. Only problem? The moonlit water was too pretty to fit her agitated mood.

After a few gulps of wine, she picked her way along the trees at the edge of the property. The heel on her right shoe snapped as she stumbled on a tree root, and she barely kept herself from falling. *Perfect*. She took the betraying shoe in her hand and glared at it.

She couldn't even storm out of a party successfully these days. She was an utter, complete failure. A professional, romantic, familial, social failure. A sour taste rose up in her throat at the realization.

As if to underscore that fact, laughter drifted across the lawn from the ballroom, taunting her. She didn't fit in with her own family. That was supposed to be the one thing every person could fall back on—family. Jade was horrified at the amount of fear and self-loathing welling up inside of her. She didn't know what to do with it. It was too big, too bitter and too scary.

She was still holding the broken shoe in one hand. Without giving it any thought, Jade smacked it against the nearest tree, as hard as she could.

That…actually felt pretty good.

She took a swig of wine and swung again. A sliver of what was left of the heel went flying, along with some tree bark. Her adrenaline surged and she started to slam the shoe into the tree over and over. In some remaining sane corner of her mind, Jade knew she was being ridiculous. She didn't care. Nobody would see her having a complete breakdown all the way out here.

Jade smacked the shoe against the tree until it was nothing but a flopping, broken sole. Even then, she kept going, only vaguely aware of the tears blurring her vision or that her hand was starting to sting.

"Which one are you trying to kill—the shoe or the tree?"

The deep voice made her spin around so fast her skirt wrapped around her legs and she almost fell over. She braced herself against the tree with the hand that still clutched the broken shoe, gripping the bottle with the other. She squinted through the shadows at Whiskey Guy. There was enough moonlight to see the slightest of smiles tugging at the corner of his mouth as he spoke.

"If it's the tree, you're wasting your time. And if it's the shoe, mission accomplished. It's definitely dead."

Her chest rose and fell as if she'd just run a marathon. She blinked and looked down at the ragged remains of the shoe in her other hand.

"It was already ruined." She wasn't sure if she meant the shoe, the wedding or her life.

He nodded as if her explanation made perfect sense. Then he stepped closer and held out his hand without saying a word. She gave him the remains of the shoe. He stepped back, turned toward the lake and threw the shoe with impressive form. There was a distant splash, then silence.

Looking out at the water, she said the only thing that came to mind.

"That was half of a three-hundred-dollar pair of shoes."

He gave a sharp laugh. "I think you took care of that problem before I arrived." He was standing close enough now that she could smell his earthy cologne. Or maybe that was just him. Maybe he smelled that way all the time. His face sobered. "You're bleeding."

Eyes clearing, she looked down at her skinned knuckles and grimaced. It must have happened while she was murdering the shoe. Damn it, she couldn't even have a decent hissy fit without screwing it up. And this stranger had witnessed it. He must think she was crazy. Scratch that. He *knew* she was crazy. The last thing she needed tonight was yet another person judging her.

She fiercely pointed a shaking finger at him, and he leaned back.

"I am *not* a disaster person, okay?"

His eyes went wide at her shouted words. He looked more than a little concerned.

"O-kay…"

"I mean it. I might not have it all together, but I am not the cause of every damn thing that goes wrong in other people's lives! Hell, sometimes, I even *fix* things, but does anyone notice when that happens? Of course not! All they want to see is the mistakes. I know who I am. I know what the hell I'm doing. People should freaking *respect* me instead of shoving me into the corner so I don't ruin their pictures."

"Nobody puts Miss Sapphire in a corner. Got it.

You know that whole scene on the dance floor wasn't your fault, right? That guy deserved what you gave him." He gave her a crooked smile. "Unlike that poor shoe."

His calm demeanor took the angry wind out of her sails. Also, Whiskey Guy was downright distracting when he smiled. His lips quirked in this really interesting way, making her wonder if he was as talented with his mouth as he was with his throwing hand. She had a hunch *his* kisses wouldn't be sloppy or gross or unwelcome. And he'd just *defended* her. When's the last time anyone had done that? Not that she was a damsel in distress or anything, but still. It was nice.

No, not nice. *Nice* was the wrong word. Nice was polite. This wasn't niceness. It was *kindness*. Warm, unquestioning and nonjudgmental.

All her life, she'd been trying to prove to her family that she was worth including. Deep down, she still believed that if she could just show them how hard she was trying to fit in, or make herself useful, or let them say whatever they wanted and keep smiling…maybe then, they would give her their love and acceptance without constantly threatening to take it back the moment she misbehaved or failed to live up to their standards. She was fighting a losing battle— love she had to fight for wasn't love at all.

Her anger evaporated. Which was a shame, because it was apparently the only thing keeping her upright. Her knees started to buckle, and Whiskey quickly stepped forward.

"I've got you, slugger. There we go. Kick off that other shoe. That's it." He slid his arm around her waist and guided her to a picnic table near the shoreline. And because she was tired and lost and he had a great smile, she figured, what the hell?

Just this once, she'd allow herself to rely on the kindness of strangers.

Chapter Two

Trent Michaels looked at the woman sitting next to him on the picnic table, her head on his shoulder, his jacket wrapped around her. This wasn't how he'd seen this evening going, but he had no complaints. He'd been wondering if it was too soon to politely head back to his room when he saw Sapphire on the dance floor, her body language screaming unhappiness. The only name he had for her was Sapphire Seduction—the first thing they'd talked about. The man she'd been dancing with grabbed a handful of her bottom. Trent could tell she was ticked off about it.

Hell, *he* was ticked off, too. Then the guy pulled her in and attempted some sort of sloppy kiss. That, and her disgusted expression, propelled Trent toward the dance floor. Before he could get there, Sapphire sent the guy flying backward with a hard check to the shoulders. The shove sent him into the newly-weds, and into the waiter and his tray of bright blue drinks. That's when Trent caught the jerk and got him back on his unsteady feet.

In the ensuing chaos, caused more by the scream-ing bride than anything else, he'd lost Sapphire. He'd been out on the veranda when she went past him in a blur of blue satin, with a shattered look in her eyes. She was clutching a half-empty wine bottle, and he felt honor-bound to follow. He wanted to be sure she didn't accidentally end up in the lake. He'd keep a respectful distance and make sure she was safe, without infringing on her privacy. That was the plan, anyway.

But then she lost her composure against that tree. No matter how many times Trent reminded himself that this was not his business, and she wasn't some-one he had a right to defend—because, as his sister was always telling him, *not all women want to be rescued, jackass*—he couldn't help watching. He wished someone she knew had come looking for her, but no one seemed to miss her.

Dark mountains sat like hulking shadows around the perimeter of Gallant Lake. This was the sort of place where he'd imagined himself ending up when he'd been in school. This was what he'd pursued a law degree to protect—nature in its purest form. He hadn't worked all those years to end up in a corporate law firm that defended businesses looking to destroy vistas like this. Yet somehow that's where he'd landed, at Bennett, Bradley and Baxter, using his knowledge of environmental law to help corporations stay out of trouble. The firm also represented the business owned by the groom's family, which was why Trent was here. He was the lucky one chosen to represent the firm. Probably payback for skipping out on last month's team-building retreat.

Somewhere, an owl hooted in the night. Another answered from a tree nearby. He used to tell himself he was *still* protecting the environment, just from within the belly of the beast. A regular Robin Hood or whatever. But that line was getting more difficult to swallow whenever he looked in the mirror.

Sapphire sniffled, then sat up abruptly, as if she'd just realized she had her head on his shoulder. She was tall—he was six-four, and she was just a few inches shy of that once she'd kicked off her shoes. She had the lean, strong build of an athlete. She had the swing of one too, with the way she'd destroyed her shoe against the tree. He bit back a grin. She'd been very focused during her little temper tantrum— she'd been biting her lower lip so hard he was surprised it wasn't bleeding. Her ebony hair was pulled back into a tight knot, but a few long tendrils had broken free.

She wiped her damp cheek hurriedly with the back

of her hand, pulling her shoulders back with a grim smile.

"I'm not usually like this, I swear. It's been an exceptionally bad day."

"So you don't make a habit of attacking trees with your shoe?"

She huffed a soft laugh. "That was definitely a first. I can't afford to destroy expensive footwear on a regular basis." She saw the wine bottle she was still clutching in her hand and held it up as if she had no idea where it came from. "Did I drink all of this?"

She didn't show any signs of being under the influence. "The bottle was open when you grabbed it off the bar, and I think you spilled more than you drank."

She set it on the table next to her. "I'm doing all sorts of things tonight I don't normally do. My therapist will pay off her mortgage from this weekend's stories alone."

Trent liked her openness. She seemed…genuine. It was refreshing. She'd let her guard down, and he had the feeling it was something she didn't do very often.

"Well," he answered, "I think I've already paid for *my* therapist's house. We're working on his beach condo now." Or they would be, if he ever made it to an appointment. It had been six months.

Her eyes went wide, and so did her smile. "Therapist buddies. I like it." She tipped her head slightly.

"Should we list our phobias and obsessions to see if we're a match? I fear rejection. How about you?"

Yeah…he wasn't going there. "I can't believe you get rejected all that often, Sapphire."

Her smile faded. "You said that before. Why Sapphire?"

"Your blue dress. And the drink earlier… Sapphire Seduction."

Her nose wrinkled. "Sounds like a stripper name." She laughed softly to herself. "Maybe I should go tell my family that's my new career path, since the old one isn't working out very well."

His chest tightened. He could relate to the career issues. Another connection between them.

"I know what it's like to be in the wrong job. And the wrong family." By marriage, anyway. "Maybe it's time to introduce ourselves properly. I'm…"

She stopped him by placing two fingers against his mouth. Her touch did more than stop his words. It stopped his breath. His heart. His ability to think.

"Don't tell me. I've already named you Whiskey Guy. For tonight, I think Sapphire and Whiskey work just fine. Don't you?"

He cupped her hand in his, holding her fingers pressed against his lips. Maybe it was the moonlight. Maybe it was the whiskey. Or all those little connections running between them like silk threads, drawing them closer. Or maybe it was the way her eyes went wide when he kissed her fingertips. The move surprised him, too. But damn, it all felt right. He swallowed hard.

"I don't make a habit of picking up tree-beating women whose names I don't know, but in your case, I'm willing to make an exception."

Her answering laughter was unfiltered, straight from the gut, and incredibly sexy. She leaned a little closer. "I don't know about you, but I have no interest in going back inside."

He thought her eyes were intoxicating before, but when they went all soft and inviting, he felt a surge of adrenaline rush through his veins. Was she suggesting what he thought she was suggesting?

"Well, Sapphire, if you want to come up to my room…we could…talk or…whatever you feel like doing. No real names required."

She grinned. "Well, Whiskey, I don't make a habit of following strange nameless men to their hotel rooms, but…" She held up the bottle in a mock toast. "In your case, I might be willing to make an exception."

Sapphire stood, her remaining shoe dangling from her fingers. She was steady on her feet now, and her eyes seemed clear, but his conscience made him ask.

"Are you sure? I mean, we won't do anything we don't *both* want to do, but are you…?"

"Too drunk to make good decisions?" Her smile was sardonic. "I think I've already proven that I don't need to be drinking to make bad choices. Turns out attacking a tree really burns off some alcohol. I'm sober." She took a step toward him and slid her hand up his chest. For a moment, he forgot what they were talking about. "But your chivalry is noted. Any other concerns?"

"No, ma'am. Not unless…" Oh right, there was something. "That guy you were dancing with before, was he your—"

"No! God, no." Her nose scrunched up, and she tugged his jacket more snuggly around her. "He's nothing to me, and even if he had been, after tonight he'd be toast. I'm single. And you?"

He was permanently single. "I'm…very free."

She studied him in the moonlight. The music and laughter from the ballroom made it clear the wedding guests were doing the "Cupid Shuffle" line dance.

Trent felt like he was doing his own version of a shuffle, and he wasn't really sure who was supposed to take the next step. Sapphire had been pushed around enough tonight, so he'd let her set the pace.

She slid her arm through his, already pulling him toward the hotel.

"Let's go, Whiskey. The night isn't getting any younger, and we have so much to…um…*talk* about."

Trent was more than happy to follow.

Chapter Three

Downtown Gallant Lake was far busier than Jade had expected this early on a Sunday morning. The plan was to find the local bakery, grab some comfort food, then slink back to her room at the resort and lay low. *Really* low. Walk-of-shame low.

She adjusted her sunglasses. The actual walk of shame had been at four o'clock that morning, when she'd slipped out of Whiskey's room and ran to her own, wearing her blue evening dress and nothing else. If anyone had seen her, makeup blurred and hair loose down her back, they'd have had no doubt what she'd been up to. Luckily, normal people weren't strolling the hallways at that hour. Only fools like her, fleeing the scene of the craziest sex she'd ever had.

Just thinking about it made her blush as she walked along the sidewalk, avoiding eye contact with the folks walking by, thankful for her over-sized sunglasses. Whiskey knew what he was doing in the bedroom, that's for sure. From his low, rumbling voice to his gentle—and talented—fingers, the man had made her melt like warm butter, then lit her up like a torch. It shouldn't have been as surprising, or as life-changing, as it was.

But…hot damn.

Things had started awkwardly. When he'd closed the door of his suite behind them, she'd had second thoughts. Jade wasn't a one-night stand kind of woman, especially with a total stranger. She didn't even know his *name*! Once they were alone together, all the reasons it might be a bad idea ran through her mind. Whiskey must have seen her doubts, because he'd promptly unlocked the dead bolt and stepped back.

"Just wanna be extra clear. Nothing happens that we aren't *both* one hundred percent on board with. If you just want to vent, I'm happy to listen. I've got a bottle of scotch I bought earlier, but there's also water, soda, whatever you want." He gestured toward the dresser and minifridge. "We can exchange names, or not." He sat on the sofa—not the bed—and patted the cushion next to him. "Let's start here, okay?"

They'd shared a quiet drink, fingers slowly becoming entwined between them. A few low words. A tentative, teasing kiss. And another. And then hands roamed, zippers unzipped and cushions hit the floor. Their clothing soon followed. They made it to the bed eventually, finally falling asleep in a tangle of arms and legs and warm skin against skin. When she'd slipped away a few hours later, pulling on her dress and rushing back to her own bed, he'd barely moved from his deep slumber. Back in her room, Jade hadn't slept a wink. How could she, with the memories of their lovemaking fresh and hot on her mind? She couldn't forget any of it if she tried. And yet…she would never even know his name.

"Excuse me, are you looking for something?" An elderly man's voice brought her back to morning, standing on the sidewalk in Gallant Lake. At first, she was startled and on guard, but the stranger looked up at her with a kind smile and warm gray eyes. "You seem like you might be lost. I've lived here all my life, so I'm betting I can send you in the right direction if you give me a name or place." He held out his hand. "Carl Wallace." He pointed at the sign above the nearby storefront. "Wallace Liquors is the family business. My daughter runs it now, though. I'm semiretired."

Jade smiled. That was a lot of information included with a friendly handshake. Things were different in small towns, she supposed. On the busy streets of St. Louis, people wouldn't have paid any attention to whether she looked lost or not, as long as she didn't block their path. She slid off her sunglasses and smiled.

"I was actually looking for the local bakery?"

He shook his head. "The bakery closed up five years ago. Building's for sale down on the corner. You've got two options. The grocery store outside of town has baked goods, or the Gallant Brew coffee shop a few doors that way has some pastries and the like. My wife Cathy works there. They have 'em brought in from the next town every morning."

"Okay. Thanks. There's really no local bakery?" She looked at all the cars going by and the people walking along the lakeshore in the quaint resort town. "Maybe I should move here and open one."

As soon as she said the flippant words—truly meant as a joke—out loud, the idea took root and started to grow. It was a crazy idea. Almost as crazy as a wild night of sex with a nameless stranger, a little voice in her head whispered. And look how good *that* turned out. Shaking off another wave of tingles, Jade smiled at how bold she was feeling in Gallant Lake. Almost shameless. There must be something in the air here in this little mountain town.

Carl's owlish eyes went even brighter with interest. "Oh! Do you bake?"

Did she *bake*? She'd won awards in culinary school, where she'd landed after she blew out her knee playing college basketball. Her Greek cream-filled bougatsa pastry had won Best Restaurant Dessert in St. Louis, right before the restaurant was sold. Other restaurants had made offers, but they all had pastry chefs, so she'd be an assistant. She wanted to be her own boss, in control of her own destiny.

She smiled at Carl. "Yes, I can bake. Pretty well, actually."

Carl nodded. "I'll tell you what, this town is growing fast. I reckon it could support a local bakery again, if you're serious." He reached for her arm, politely waiting for permission. When she nodded, he gently linked arms and started walking with her, leading her down the street like they were already friends. "Let me introduce you to Nora at the coffee shop. She's involved with a group of women entrepreneurs in the area. If we're lucky, Brittany Thomas will be in there, too, getting her morning coffee. She's a local real estate broker who might be able to get you in to look at the old bakeshop."

Jade was glad she'd opted for flats this morning, so she didn't tower over the old guy too much. "That's so nice of you! But… I mean… You don't even know me, Carl. What makes you think I can even *run* a bakery?"

His wise eyes twinkled. "I know a thing or two about strong women. I raised one, and I've been married to two. You've got the look of someone ready for a fresh start in a place like this. Fresh starts are hard to come by, but not impossible."

She felt the need to slow him down before things got out of hand. "I'm really only in town for a wedding." *And a hot night with a stranger.* "I go home tomorrow." *Home to no job, no boyfriend and a family where I'm the square peg that will clearly never fit in.* "And I don't know if I have enough cash to start a business from scratch."

Jade wasn't sure why she was spilling all this tea with a stranger, especially after she'd already shared so much with another stranger the night before. It definitely wasn't like her to trust people this easily.

But Carl's hand was already on the door to the coffee shop, and he only stopped long enough to face her with a wry smile. "Where's home?"

"St. Louis."

Carl nodded. "Big city. You might find things a bit more affordable here." With that, he pulled the door open and held it for her while she entered. An older woman standing behind the counter immediately welcomed Carl with an affectionate wave. Her gray hair hung over her shoulder in a long braid. Another woman, petite with a brunette bob, was busy with customers, but nodded their way with a wink.

Carl said this was a place where people made fresh starts, and that was just what Jade was looking for. Away from her family and all the comparisons and head games and insecurity about her position as an outsider.

The brunette turned out to be the owner of the

shop, Nora Peyton. She wiped her hands on her apron as Carl made introductions, then led Jade to a window table.

"If you're serious about opening a bakery here, I'd be your first customer." Nora's smile was bright as she patted Jade's hand. "It's at the top of our business owner group's wish list. That and a restaurant downtown, but I want a bakery for purely selfish reasons. I'm tired of getting my pastries from two towns away. If the weather's bad, they don't always get here, and then my husband has to go get them and…"

As Nora rattled on about how awesome it would be, the idea took more solid shape in Jade's mind. Nora said the business group could line her up with loans or grants, funded by the resort's owner, who happened to be married to Nora's cousin. That must be another small-town thing—everyone knew everyone. Was that what she wanted?

She watched the customers coming into the coffee shop as Nora talked. They checked the community bulletin board. They admired the artwork for sale on the wall. They greeted each other warmly. There were young couples and seniors. Skin in every shade. The group at the table next to them was laughing and talking rapidly in what sounded like an Eastern European language.

A small town, but not one that felt isolated from the world at large. Still…uprooting her life (such as it was) to move to little Gallant Lake, which she'd been in for all of thirty-six hours? Did that make sense?

No doubt she'd think of Whiskey and their night together every time she saw the resort. But he'd mentioned catching a flight back to Denver today, so it's not like she'd ever see him again.

And she'd be putting distance between herself and her perpetually-disappointed family. Which made this idea make more sense. What better way to make a fresh start than to do it in a place where no one knew her? Where no one knew she was the woman who never fit in?

She interrupted Nora's proud description of the new businesses opening here on Main Street.

"Do you think you could call that real estate friend of yours?"

Chapter Four

Mid October...

"This weekend was a smashing success, Jade." Nora lifted a cup of tea in a toast as Jade locked the front door of The Sweet Greek Bakery. "A grand opening to remember!"

Nora's cousins, Amanda Randall and Mel Brannigan, raised their cups, too. The three "Lowery women," as they called themselves, were at the table nearest the glass display counter. Amanda's husband, Blake, owned the big resort. Mel had a designer boutique on Main Street, and Nora, of course, owned the Gallant Brew three doors down. Movers and shakers in little Gallant Lake. Jade leaned back against the now-locked door and closed her eyes in relief. And exhaustion.

It had taken a couple of months to purchase the building once Nora connected Jade with real estate agent Brittany Thomas. Remodeling and upgrading the cafe and kitchen had taken even more time, and nearly all of her grandmother's inheritance. Convincing her family that she was really, truly leaving St. Louis for Gallant Lake? Well, that was an ongoing challenge.

Marla didn't seem to care one way or the other, but Dad had plenty of reservations. She'd never run her own business. She knew nothing about—and no one *in*—Gallant Lake. But she'd assured him it was going to be fine. After all, she'd made it this far in Project Fresh Start, even after being blindsided in the middle of the process with news that changed everything.

She looked at her three new friends and smiled, doing her best to look happy, which she was, and energized, which she definitely was not. She brushed her hand down the front of her long apron, wondering how long she'd be able to hide her news behind aprons and baggy clothes. "I couldn't have done it without you ladies and your connections. The Sweet Greek Bakery is off to a great start thanks to you." She joined them at the table. "Your connections brought people in all weekend long. I sold out of almost everything. It's a good thing I'm closed on Mondays, just so I can restock."

Nora waved her forefinger. "It wasn't us—it was your *baking* skills that brought people in, and *kept* them here. I swear, those little bird's nest things… what did you call them?"

"Kunafa nests."

"Yes! Those things were so damn good—people were going crazy for them!"

"I sold out both days," Jade agreed. "Today the after-church crowd was taking them home by the boxful." The crunchy little baked nests of kataifah pastry, which looked like shredded wheat, were wrapped around a few pecans, like eggs in a nest.

"This baklava…" Amanda popped one last small bite in her mouth. "To *die* for!"

"And it wasn't just the fancy Mediterranean stuff," Mel said. "Those brown butter cookies…*ridiculous*, Jade."

Jade wasn't used to being blanketed with compliments. She was tempted to brush them off and say things weren't *that* good. But damn it, she *was* a good pastry chef. And this *had* been a spectacular grand opening weekend. So she smiled and simply said "Thank you."

"And it's so pretty in here!" Nora looked around. "I feel happy just walking inside."

Jade had taken her decorating advice from Amanda, who was an interior designer. She wanted the bakery to reflect her mother's heritage. The walls and floors were bright white, with the back wall and curtains a brilliant Mediterranean blue. Along the back wall was a blue-tiled counter topped with five chrome spigots that dispensed near-boiling water. Boxes of teas were available to select from.

She'd never intended to have a dine-in area, but Amanda convinced her to have at least a few small tables where people could enjoy a treat. Nora already had a coffee shop and Jade didn't want to compete, so the tea counter was born.

Nora left the table, and returned with a cup of tea for Jade. She noticed Jade staring at the dark brew. "Don't worry, it's decaf."

"Oh, good." Jade had taken her first sip before she realized what had just happened. She set the mug down, her pulse quickening. "I mean…um…not that it matters if it's…decaf…or not…"

The three cousins were each so different—Nora was petite, with short, dark hair. Amanda was petite but curvier, with blond curls falling down her back. And Mel, a former model, was tall and statuesque like Jade. But right now, they were all staring back at her with identical expressions. Each wore a slightly sympathetic but knowing smile, their eyes warm with concern and a little bit of laughter.

"Really?" Nora asked. "Your doctor hasn't told you to avoid caffeine?" Her face fell. "You *are* seeing a doctor, right?"

A small chill raced down Jade's spine. So much for her secret. Amanda leaned back and ran her eyes down Jade's frame. "I'm guessing it's still pretty early. Four months? Five?"

Mel shook her head. "You're both forgetting how tall she is. I didn't start showing much until at least five months, so I'm guessing five or six?"

Jade's hand went to her stomach, rounded and firm under the camouflage. The game was up.

"How long have you known?" she whispered. Was the whole town talking about her?

"I suspected in August," Nora answered, "when you suddenly started ordering decaf coffee."

"I noticed last month," Mel snickered. "You had a peculiar shade of green to your skin tone in the mornings, and I remember having that same lovely tint after hugging the porcelain throne every morning when I was expecting Patrick and Bonnie."

Amanda put her hand on her chest. "I confess I totally missed it until these two pointed it out a few weeks ago. I told them they were crazy, because there was no way you'd have the energy to open a brand-new business while pregnant." She shook her head. "And yet, there you were, working all those long hours with that aching back you kept rubbing." Amanda put her hand on Jade's. "How far along?"

"Six months." She swallowed hard. "Does everyone know?"

"I don't know about *everyone*, but most of your

friends know—or at least suspect." Amanda patted her hand. "You've done a good job of hiding that baby bump with your baggy tops and long aprons, but you won't be able to hide it much longer. What's your plan?"

Jade's silence filled the bakery. She'd buried herself in the bakery to *avoid* coming up with a plan, but she was six months pregnant. Denial was no longer a viable option. Keeping it a secret served no purpose at this point...if it ever had.

"Well..." She shrugged, finally looking up to meet their worried faces. "I guess I'm going to have a baby—" she glanced at Nora "—and yes, I have a doctor. Everything's fine. It's a girl."

A chorus of *awwws* went around the table. Jade grinned, surprised how happy she was to talk about it. "I'm calling her Bunny for now—you know, my bun in the oven?"

"That is the cutest thing I've ever heard," Amanda sighed.

"And you're doing this alone by choice?" Mel asked. "No dad?"

Oh, there was a dad, alright. A tall, handsome blond with golden eyes and a smile that had flashed bright in the moonlight along the lakeshore six months ago. A man whose hands had been her balm on one very stressful night. A man who'd rocked her world, and, despite their precautions, had left her with a lifelong souvenir. Her hand rubbed her stomach lightly. A man who had no idea she was carrying his daughter.

"Dad's not in the picture," she answered. At least not yet. Maybe never. She hadn't decided yet.

"Okay," Nora started, "but just to clarify—you are *not* doing this alone. You live in Gallant Lake now, and no one has to face anything alone in this town."

Jade somehow managed not to shed any tears as the Lowery cousins circled her with a group hug before they left. She knew they meant it when they said they'd be there for her. She just wasn't *used* to that kind of support. It left her awkwardly thanking them while telling them she didn't need help, even when they all knew she did. They had parenting knowledge Jade was going to need. At the same time, she couldn't help *resenting* her need. Her independent streak was going to trip her up again if she wasn't careful.

After locking up the bakery, she headed home and walked up the metal fire escape stairs to the apartment she'd rented from Nora. The charming loft was above the coffee shop. It would have been nice to live directly above her shop, but the two floors above the bakery had been converted long ago into storage space and a third-floor office. She needed both, so, at least for now, using Nora's vacant apartment kept her close enough to walk to the shop in the predawn hours to begin baking.

The loft had been completely updated when Nora

lived there. It was stylish and upscale, with the original brick walls and two stories of windows overlooking Gallant Lake and Main Street. She climbed another set of industrial stairs inside the apartment to reach the master suite in the loft. In a few months' time, that climb was going to be even more exhausting than it was now. And the bare metal railing at the edge of the loft was *not* child-safe in any way.

Jade fell back on the bed and reminded herself not to doom-spiral. This apartment was lovely, furnished and inexpensive. The baby would sleep in a bassinet near Jade's bed for her first few months, and wouldn't be walking for months after that. She had time. There were rental houses in town. She might even find a small home she could afford to *buy*, assuming the bakery was successful.

The grand opening weekend made that success more likely. There had been lines out the door both days, and business had been brisk during her soft opening the week before. The Greek pastries were an absolute hit, and the regular bakery fare—cakes, cookies, cupcakes—all sold strongly as well. Which meant she was going to need to hire some help. Her chest tightened, and she had to remind herself again to relax. Her OB/GYN had warned her to limit her stress.

That made Jade laugh out loud, lying there alone in her bedroom loft. She was having a *baby*. How on earth was she supposed to limit her stress when she was *having a baby*? She took a deep breath, held it, then released it slowly. Then did it again. And again. Until she finally felt her pulse slowing.

She'd been almost three months along before she'd even noticed she was carrying a child. To be fair, she'd never been the most regular of women anyway. With the stress of losing her job, her half sister's wedding and the impulsive decision to start fresh here in Gallant Lake, she hadn't even noticed the first missed period. The second missed one got her attention, but she was in the midst of negotiating on the bakery purchase, so she'd chalked that up to stress and exhaustion. It never occurred to her that one foolish night with Whiskey Guy had resulted in pregnancy...until she started throwing up every morning and realized she'd missed her *third* period in a row.

A doctor had confirmed the four store-bought pregnancy test results. She was pregnant. *Really* pregnant. She didn't need another complication in the middle of restarting her life. But...this complication was *hers*. Her child. She'd *belong* to this child as much as the child would belong to her. And the decision made itself—she was having this baby.

Which meant that Trent Michaels was having a baby, too. But he didn't know it. Not yet, anyway. She glanced at her laptop on the nightstand, then sat up and opened it. The draft email was right there, in the same folder it had been sitting in for three weeks.

Unsent. It hadn't been that hard to find Trent's identity. There were only so many people at the reception.

A few well-timed, casual inquiries to different people so no one got suspicious, and there he was—Trent Michaels, a partner at the law firm her new brother-in-law's family used. She'd never see the guy again. Unless she told him she was having his baby. Then she might be seeing him a lot. Which was why the email was still sitting in her drafts folder.

Their daughter...*her* daughter...wasn't due until January. Plenty of time to tell him. That was, *if* Jade decided to tell him. She kept telling herself she could raise this child alone. The question was...*should* she?

Hiding the pregnancy from people had just sort of happened. She'd been so overwhelmed at the news that she'd wanted time to figure things out on her own—the way she'd always done. But motherhood wasn't meant to be handled alone, and she had no idea how she was going to do this.

Some days she doubted whether she should be doing *any* of the things she was doing. Moving. Opening a bakery. Bringing a baby into the world. Was Gallant Lake the fresh start she needed? Only time would tell, and she couldn't change any of it now.

Trent saw his name as soon as he got to the luggage area of JFK. He'd expected to have to hunt down a shuttle to the environmental conference.

The older man holding the sign smiled at Trent. "Gallant Lake Resort, Mr. Michaels?"

"Yes. I…are you the shuttle driver?"

The man chuckled. "I'm Stewart, and this is your lucky day. The resort owner was flying home today, and Mr. Randall asked us to check to see if any guests were arriving around the same time so he could offer transportation. At no charge to you, of course. There's already another gentleman waiting in the limo with Mr. Randall. Did you check any bags?"

"Thanks, Stewart. And yes, I checked a bag." He noticed a familiar black suitcase with a bright blue strap securing it. "There it is—" He'd taken a step toward the moving conveyor, but Stewart stopped him.

"I have it, sir." He grabbed the bag and extended the handle. "Follow me, Mr. Michaels."

Trent hesitated, then followed as ordered. It wasn't Stewart's fault that he'd been hoping this trip would get him *away* from all the corporate trappings of his job. He just wanted to be plain old Trent while he was in Gallant Lake this week, getting back to his low-key environmentalist roots for a few days at the conference. A chance to examine where his life was heading and whether he wanted to stay on his current career track or not. A limo ride to the resort with its probably stuffy old owner wasn't exactly part of that plan. It would be like catching a ride with his boss, Leonard Baxter, back home in Colorado.

Leonard couldn't go five minutes without bragging about his mountainside mansion, his Vail condo, his fancy car, his expensive cigars, and on and on and on. Leonard told one of the other partners that he bragged in order to inspire the staff to work harder. He assumed everyone wanted the life he had.

There was a time when Trent had been seduced by the idea. Or at least his ex-wife had been, and he'd wanted to make Cindy happy. But Cindy left two years ago, and Trent was still stuck at Bennett, Bradley and Baxter, doing profitable, but mind-numbingly boring, corporate law.

He steeled himself as he approached the gleaming black SUV that Stewart was putting his luggage into. The resort was at least a ninety-minute drive from the city. *Perfect*...

The first thing that greeted Trent as he opened the back door to the extended SUV was loud laughter. The next was the scent of expensive booze...*scotch*, if his nose was accurate. He checked his watch—it was barely noon.

Inside the vehicle, two men, probably in their mid-forties, were laughing and toasting each other with heavy lead crystal glasses.

"Here's to baby girls!" A tall, dark-haired man was lifting his glass high. The sandy-haired man across from him wore a big grin.

"Thanks, Blake. I'm still in shock."

The first guy gestured for Trent to come in. "Make yourself comfortable. Vince just found out he and his wife are having a baby girl after having three boys, so I had to do a toast. I know it's early, but I'm making them short, so I promise you won't be impaired when you get to Gallant Lake. I'm Blake Randall, by the way." He extended his hand, and Trent took it. *So much for a stuffy old guy.*

"Trent Michaels. Thanks for the ride, Mr. Randall. It was a nice surprise." He nodded to the decanter of scotch. "I'd be happy to join you. Congratulations, Vince."

Blake took another glass and splashed some golden liquid into it, handing it to Trent. "Call me Blake, and you're welcome. I figured as long as I was here, I'd pick up a couple guests. After all, this is supposed to be an environmentally friendly conference, so carpooling made sense. It'll be a while before anyone else arrives, so we'll be heading up now. Sit back and relax, gents."

The time flew by as the three men talked about the Catskills, the resort and the conference. Trent had to fight for permission to come here from old man Baxter, and finally took vacation time after Leonard only approved a single day of a five-day conference featuring environmentalists from around the world, as well as sub-conferences of business owners, consumer organizations, carmakers and activist groups. The whole thing was the brainchild of Vincent Grassman, who headed an environmental think tank. *Wait a minute...*

"I'm sorry," Trent interrupted a conversation about the differences between raising girls and boys between Blake and Vince. "Are you Vince *Grassman*? You put this whole thing together?"

The other man smiled. "I am Vince Grassman, but I can't claim responsibility for the entire conference. I had an idea, and a team of people ran with it. Luckily, one of them talked to Blake here, and we ended up with a perfect venue." Vince tipped his head to the side. "Michaels... You're from a law firm, right? Interested in environmental law?"

Trent grimaced. "My firm is in Denver, but I'm afraid I'm the only one there interested in this subject." He lifted one shoulder. "I had to take vacation time to attend this event."

"I take it you're *not* into corporate law?" Vince asked. "Here looking for a new job, maybe?"

Trent hesitated. He knew how rabid the legal gossip grapevine could be, even 2,000 miles from home. "I'm here to expand my personal knowledge on the topic."

Vince stared for a beat, then nodded with a smile. "Understood. Let me know if you want any introductions. Confidentially, of course."

"You're using vacation time for this?" Blake shook his head. "I hope you're going to take some time to do something fun. The concierge at the resort will be glad to give you some suggestions. Of course, our little town isn't as exciting as a city like Denver."

"I brought some climbing gear," Trent said. "I'm hoping to get a chance to hit the Gunks." The Shawangunk Mountains were famous for their sheer climbing face—one of the best in the East. "It's actually not my first time in Gallant Lake. I was here for a wedding back in April, but that was a quick trip."

And the best sex of his life. Trent smiled to himself. He wondered what Sapphire was up to these days? Did she still think of their night together as often, and as fondly, as he did? Did he haunt her dreams the way she did his?

He'd never indulged in a nameless night of passion like that before, and he wasn't sure if it was the secrecy that made it so hot, or if they were just that good together. It was a memory to be treasured. Even if he *was* a little worried that no other woman would ever live up to what the two of them had shared that special night.

"You climb?" Blake asked. "My director of security is a climber. Nick goes to the Gunks all the time. I'll make sure you two meet this afternoon."

Trent thanked Blake as the conversation turned to environmentally friendly initiatives the resort was taking. Trent tried to focus, but his thoughts kept jumping back to the night that rocked his world. He'd thought about finding out her name—it wouldn't be that difficult. Every time he was tempted, he reminded himself that part of the intrigue of their night together was the anonymity. Two strangers on a moonlit night, coming together like gasoline and a match. Reproducing that kind of onetime passion would be impossible, so why even try? Finding her in real life—in *daylight*—might tarnish the memory of their night.

By the time the limo reached the resort, the three men had agreed to meet over dinner that night, and Blake had texted his pal Nick to put together a climb with Trent. The limo pulled into a gated property Trent didn't recognize, and Blake explained it was his home, next door to the resort. His "home" turned out to be an honest-to-God *castle*, turrets and all.

"This is Halcyon. I used to call it a pile of rocks," he explained with a proud grin, "but my Amanda made it into a home. See you guys tonight at the restaurant." As Blake stepped out of the SUV, a young girl—maybe seven or eight—came running out the front door, screaming "Daddy!" Blake swung the little blonde up into his arms and around in a circle, his face beaming. Trent's skin went tight as he remembered being welcomed home like that. Something that would never happen again.

"You married? Have kids?" Vince asked as the limo headed back down the driveway.

"Nope. I'm very single." He tried to say it with enthusiasm. *Yay, I'm thirty-eight and free as a bird!* But he knew he hadn't pulled it off when he saw the pity in Vince's eyes. The married guy who was expecting his fourth child. Trent shrugged and explained.

"I was married, but it didn't work out. I'm not sure a family is in the cards for me."

Vince just laughed. "I said the same thing in my thirties. And into my forties. Then I fell head over heels for the sassy young barista at my local coffee shop in Seattle, and here I am at forty-eight, about to be a happily married father of four." He reached for the door when the vehicle stopped in front of the resort. "Life comes at you fast sometimes."

Trent got settled in his suite overlooking a bright blue Gallant Lake, surrounded by mountains covered in burnished golds and browns. These weren't the jagged peaks he was used to in Colorado. The Catskills were more rounded in shape. Everything was smaller here.

He hadn't seen much of this place in April, but Gallant Lake had struck him then as nothing more than a tourist town. "Quaint" wasn't exactly Trent's style, but he wasn't looking to move here, just enjoy the area for a week while he regrouped mentally.

As planned, he met Vince and Blake for dinner at Gallante, the resort's restaurant. The security guy, Nick West, joined them, quizzing Trent about his experience level at rock climbing. Trent didn't take offense to the questions. Climbing with some amateur who claimed a better skill level than he possessed was not fun, and it could be dangerous. Once Nick was satisfied that Trent wasn't all talk, he promised to set up a few climbs that week, including a quick one the next morning.

Back in his room later, Trent received a text from his boss. So much for being on vacation.

L: You're in New York, right?

T: I'm in the Catskills. On vacation.

L: I may need you to work.

Trent scowled at his phone. *That's not how vacations work, Leonard.* He tapped a response.

T: What's up?

L: We have a client near Albany having zoning issues with the locals. Thought you might take a meeting or two. I'll email you the file to review.

Damn it. A *meeting or two* was way too undefined for him. Which is exactly why Leonard had used the loosey-goosey wording.

T: I'll review it. As you know, I'm here to attend a conference I've paid for personally, so as long as it doesn't interfere with the schedule.

L: If it does, we'll reimburse you for what you miss.

That wasn't Trent's point, and Leonard knew it. He didn't bother responding, knowing the wheels were already in motion. Leonard was either oblivious to Trent's vacation time, or was making a power play by trampling on it. Probably a combination of both. The old guy knew how to play the corporate game better than just about anyone else Trent had ever met.

He woke early the next morning still annoyed. He'd really wanted this week to be an escape from the three-piece-suit lifestyle that had been chafing him for years. And, of course, it was raining, which killed his plans to go for a climb with Nick West. Irritation was bubbling right under his skin. He made a cup of coffee in the room, then decided to take a run and shake off his mood. The first meet-and-greet of the conference wasn't until that evening. Vince had offered to make some introductions, and Trent was ready to take him up on it.

He pulled a waterproof jacket over his T-shirt and running pants, and headed out the side door of the resort. Baxter wasn't the only one who could pull a power play. Let the gossip run all the way back to Denver that Trent Michaels was putting out feelers to law firms. Maybe then they'd take him seriously when he said he wanted to expand the firm's clientele. To take on more social and environmental concerns, maybe even some pro bono clients. Shake the rust off their staid reputation as industry attorneys.

Give him some cases he could get excited about, instead of protecting fat-cat CEOs.

Would he actually make a move? Probably not. But the thought of rattling everyone's cages a little made him smile. He ran along a path that wrapped around the resort's golf course and followed the lakeshore toward town, connecting to a small park before depositing him on Main Street. It was still early, and only a couple shops were open. The coffee shop, Gallant Brew. And a bakery a few doors down—The Sweet Greek Bakery. He promised himself he'd swing into one of them on his way back. First, he needed to work up a good sweat and clear his head.

He picked up his pace, nodding at the guy opening the local hardware store and heading back out of town toward the eastern shore of the lake. He checked his watch. He'd only run a mile so far—after another three, he'd turn around and stop for coffee and a snack when he came back through town. After that, he'd be ready to face the day.

Chapter Five

Jade boxed up three dozen cookies and handed them to Mackenzie Adams. Mack owned the liquor store just down the block, and was having a wine tasting event later where she wanted to serve Jade's brown butter cookies. The simple recipe had quickly become a bestseller in the bakery's first weeks.

Mack took the box with a grin. "These cookies are *perfect* for wine tasting." Her thick blond hair was tugged back in a ponytail, and she was wearing a puffy down coat over sweatpants. It was one of the things Jade already liked about her business—people showed up in whatever to make their purchases—no pretense at all.

That made her feel comfortable in her own fairly shapeless clothing and loose apron. It wasn't so much that she didn't want people knowing, but she wanted people talking about her *baking*, not her belly. Just then, little Bunny sent a fluttering wave across her stomach that made her jump.

Mack's eyes sparkled. "Let me guess…the little one is saying *good morning*?"

Jade nodded. "It's ten o'clock. This is usually when she tells me it's time to sit down for a few minutes."

Mack knew about the baby. So did her husband, police chief Dan Adams. And the husbands of the three Lowery cousins. And Nate, the hardware guy across the street, and his wife, Brittany. Might be time to face the fact that it wasn't a secret at all anymore.

"I agree with baby," Mack said, "it's time for you to get off your feet. Add two teas to my tab, and come sit with me for a minute."

Jade looked around the empty shop and nodded. She'd had her usual early rush, as people stopped for a pastry, or a dozen, on their way to work. There'd be another burst of business around lunchtime. She'd decided not to stay open all day, at least not until after the baby was born and she'd added some trained staff, so the bakery closed at two every day but Friday and Saturday, when she stayed open until four.

"Have you had any luck hiring yet?" Mack must have read her mind. She'd just been thinking she couldn't sustain even *those* hours as the pregnancy progressed.

"I just hired a guy who retired from the grocery store bakery last year. And his wife might be able to work part-time. I'm just worried that if he's already retired once, he's not going to be interested in anything long-term here. But—" she patted her belly, getting another little fluttery kick from Bunny in return "—if I can convince him to work full-time for the next six months, it will get me to a point where I can train someone younger."

"Hey, don't discount the senior employees." Mack took a sip of her coffee. "Cathy's been working for Nora for years now, and my dad still covers the store for me whenever I need."

"Hopefully Joe and his wife, Pat, will work out."

"Joe Caruso? Oh, he's not that old. He's a great guy." Mack looked at her watch and stood. "Oh, shoot. I promised Dan I'd pick up his uniforms from the cleaners this morning before I open the store. I swear that man goes out of his way to crawl through mud every day—he goes through dry cleaning faster than anyone I know. I keep telling him he's the police *chief*, so he should be ordering the *other* guys to do the dirty work." She held up the box of cookies. "Come join us tonight for the wine tasting—I always have sparkling water and juice on hand."

"I can't make any promises. I fall asleep early a lot of nights." The truth was, she fell asleep almost the minute she sat down when she got home.

"Everything okay?" Mack stopped on her way to the door, worry filling her eyes.

Jade kicked herself for saying anything. She wasn't one to look for sympathy from others. "I'm fine. The doctor said my blood pressure's a little low, but it's not uncommon. I'm just in a tired phase of the pregnancy. I'll try to make it tonight."

Mack studied her for a long moment, then nodded. "Dan's ex had some blood pressure issues when she was pregnant with her second after she remarried. Scared the daylights out of Chloe when she fainted once. Have you…?" Chloe was Mack's ten-year-old stepdaughter. Jade shook her head, not mentioning how close she'd come a few times.

"I'm *fine*. I promise." She crossed her fingers behind her back. "Go get Dan's uniforms."

She'd only been in the kitchen a few minutes when she heard the bell above the front door tinkling. "Be right there!" she called out, quickly wiping her hands on a towel near the sink. The dirty baking sheets would have to wait.

The man was in wet running clothes, with a cap pulled low on his forehead, blocking his face from view. He was leaning over the pastry case. She couldn't see how tall he was, how he was built, what his face looked like—not even the color of his wet hair. And yet a tremor ran from her scalp to her toes the moment she saw him. It was an electric pulse, and she wondered if she was about to faint. But no…

she didn't hear any roaring in her ears. And her feet were steady. So steady they felt glued to the floor.

The man let out a long moan, as if falling in love with the baked goods in the display. She'd heard the sound from customers before, but coming from this guy, it reverberated through her chest in a whole new way. He straightened and looked her direction over the top of the case, and suddenly fainting was a real possibility.

His mouth fell open when his whiskey-colored eyes met hers.

"Sapphire?"

Trent's brain froze. It stopped functioning the moment he looked into those wide ebony eyes that had been showing up in his dreams for months. He couldn't compute how he could be seeing her standing in front of him. In an apron. In a bakery. In Gallant Lake. In October.

She'd said she was flying *home* to St. Louis after the wedding. That was the whole point of a one-night stand—that you never saw each other again. This was…this was breaking the rules, damn it. He blinked, not even making sense to himself.

It was definitely Sapphire—tall and olive-skinned. Even with her black hair pulled into a knot on her neck and no makeup on her face, she was stunningly beautiful. She was staring at him as if she'd seen a ghost, which made him feel a little bit better—at least they were on even ground here, both shocked into silence.

"You…" he stammered, knowing they couldn't just stare at each other forever. "You said you didn't live here… I… I don't understand."

She swayed just a little as she licked her lips.

"I *didn't* live here then." Her voice was low, breaking slightly. "I do now. But why are *you*…?"

"Well, this is awkward." Trent tried to regroup as he straightened. "I'm here for a conference at the resort. It never occurred to me that you might be here. Um…how are you?"

Lame, Trent. He didn't know what to say to a woman who'd been just as happy as him to have a quick, torrid night of lovemaking before *never seeing each other again*.

She put her hand on the counter, swaying again, her face pale. *Oh, hell.* Was she going to pass out?

"Whoa." He stepped around the counter to put his arm on her waist. "Are you okay? Come and sit."

The instant she leaned into him, he remembered every curve on her body from that night in April. Long, lean and strong. But she didn't feel strong right now. She was trembling. He guided her to a chair at one of the small tables in the shop.

"What do you need? Water? Medicine?"

"I'm okay." She breathed the words more than spoke them, as if convincing herself. "Just let me sit a minute."

He stayed kneeling at her side, in case she slid off the chair. But her cheeks started showing more color after a few seconds, and she sat straighter. Her eyes opened, but she avoided looking at him. "I'm better now, Trent. Thank you."

He moved to the chair across from her. There was a *lot* more tension in the air than there should have been. They'd had their one night and this was a shocker of a reunion, but…that wasn't exactly a crisis. The emotion rolling off her felt like fear, which made no sense.

Wait…

"Did you just call me *Trent*?" he asked. "How did you…?"

She swallowed hard, then met his eyes. She was looking stronger, and her gaze was steely now. Guarded. "It wasn't that hard—it was my half sister's wedding. I'm Jade, by the way." Her mouth twitched. "Not Sapphire."

"Your actual name is *Jade* and you let me call you *Sapphire*?"

She shrugged. "You're the one who came up with the nickname. The fact that it was another gemstone was a coincidence. You could have found my name out easily enough on your own, since you're my brother-in-law's attorney."

He shook his head. "I am *not* his attorney. The firm represents his family's company—has for decades." He decided there was nothing all that shady about her figuring out who he was. He spread his hands. "And here we are, seeing each other in the real world—work aprons and workout clothes. No expensive shoes being beat on trees, and no satin gowns or tuxedos."

She returned his smile, but she still seemed tense. Worried.

"Uh-oh." He looked around. "Is there a *Mister* Jade I should be worried about?"

"No. Nothing like that."

So she was still single. Maybe this week could include something more interesting than just the conference.

"And you live here now, in Gallant Lake? You work in a bakery?"

It seemed so cozy and domestic compared to the sophisticated, sharp-tongued woman he'd met in April.

"This felt like a good place for a fresh start. And I *own* the bakery." There was pride in her voice. The place was cute, and obviously new. Everything was gleaming and fresh. His stomach grumbled, reminding him he'd come in here for food.

"Nice place. What do you recommend?"

"For breakfast? A piece of maple pumpkin coffee cake." She started to stand, but he reached for her arm.

"Can you recommend something for dinner? Care to join me tonight?"

Her mouth opened, but she was struggling to answer. For the first time, it occurred to Trent that maybe *she* didn't have the fond memories of that night that *he* did. Whoops.

"I mean…only if you want." He was stammering again. "Just dinner. Uh…if you want to leave it as just that one night—a *great* night, I might add—then we can forget it…"

She huffed out a low laugh as she pulled away and went to get his pastry. "Forgetting that night isn't an option for me."

Trent smiled, glad he'd made an impression. She placed a mile-high square of gooey coffee cake laced with maple cinnamon swirls into a white paper bag. He saw the tea bar, but she didn't offer him any. He got the message—it was time for him to go. With*out* dinner plans, apparently. He set his money on the counter and turned to leave. He was almost out the door when she called his name.

"Trent…how long are you in town?"

"Through the weekend."

"Um…maybe we should…" She frowned, waving her hand. "Never mind."

Was she thinking about having dinner after all?

"Wanna exchange numbers?" He held up his phone.

"Nope." She shook her head emphatically. *Okay then*.

He held up the paper bag in his other hand. "This

smells amazing, by the way. If you do want to talk over cocktails, I'm at the resort. Room 314."

She licked her upper lip, looking for all the world like she wanted to say something. Instead, she turned away. "Got it."

"It was a nice surprise to see you…"

She was already heading into the back of the bakery. Done with him, from the looks of it. This encounter didn't feel like a recipe for another passionate interlude.

Chapter Six

Jade tried to focus on Mack's description of the wine she was pouring, but it was no use. With every breath, she thought of Trent. How he'd shown up that morning out of nowhere. How sexy he'd looked, all rain-soaked and sweaty in those workout clothes. The intensity of his gaze, and how she'd frozen like a deer in the headlights. The jolt of electricity she'd felt when he'd put his arm around her. At least they both knew each other's real names now.

"What are you drinking?" Mel Brannigan leaned forward to look into Jade's glass. "Oh, you were smart—the fake mimosas. I opted for the pomegranate water, and it's grossly sweet. At least you're getting some healthy orange juice out of the deal." There was a burst of laughter from the other tables, where women were sipping *real* wine. Which was something Jade would *really* like to be doing right now. She patted Bunny. *Someday.* Mel's brows lowered. "You okay, sweetie?"

"I'm fine." Jade should just tattoo that on her hand so she could hold it up whenever someone asked— *I'm fine.* "Just tired. And I'd kill for a glass of wine right now." Then she remembered that Mel was abstaining because of a substance abuse problem. "Sorry."

"No worries," Mel answered. "You're allowed to crave wine around me. I choose *not* to drink, but other drinkers don't bother me at all. Hey, do you want me to walk you home? You look beat."

"I'm fine…" Jade winced. "I know I keep saying that, but I really am. I do think I'll head home though."

"Yeah, me, too." Mel stood and did a quick finger wave to Mack, who was helping her guests select wine to purchase. "The guys are playing poker in Asher's back room, so I'll walk you that far."

Jade shook her head as she followed. Asher Peyton's woodworking shop was one door beyond her apartment above Nora's coffee shop, so Mel was effectively walking Jade home. *Welcome to Gallant Lake.* When people cared in this town, they cared one hundred percent and then some. Even for someone who constantly pushed them away, like Jade did. They just kept on caring, no matter how many times she used the word *fine*.

She was settling into bed when her phone rang. She checked the screen and groaned.

"Dad, I keep telling you New York is an hour behind St. Louis. It's late."

"It's nine thirty here, which is ten thirty there," Dad answered. "I remember when you didn't even head *out* to party until after ten thirty."

"Sure, when I was *twenty*. Not thirty-five and *pregnant*, or have you forgotten that part?" She laid her head on the pillow and closed her eyes, knowing she'd just opened the door to a lecture.

"It's kinda hard to forget my oldest daughter is having a baby all by herself in some little town on the edge of civilization."

"Dad, I'm ninety minutes from Manhattan."

"You'd never know it. The place doesn't even have a decent restaurant."

"The resort has two restaurants and we have a pizza shop and a coffee shop and an awesome new bakery." Marla had turned Jade's father into a borderline snob over the years. "You'd know that if you came to visit more often."

"Honey, you know how busy I've been at the firm. The markets are volatile right now and my clients need me."

"Your daughter needs you, too." It was pouty and manipulative, but that didn't mean it wasn't true. He'd been there twice since she'd moved. Once to help with the apartment, and just a few weeks ago to see the nearly finished bakery.

"I guess this is what I get for calling you so late. You're always grumpy when you're tired." His soft laugh softened the words. He wasn't accusing, just sharing an intimate truth that a father would know. "From now on I'll try to call you earlier, for both our sakes. How are you?"

She smiled, feeling his genuine concern. "I'm good. The grand opening went well. I've hired a guy to cover for my maternity leave. It's all coming together."

"So you put your grandmother's inheritance to good use, eh?"

"I think so. Yaya would have loved the shop." She hesitated. "So would Mom."

Jade could picture Dad looking around to make sure Marla wasn't nearby. Marla was ridiculously jealous of a dead woman. "Your mother loved to cook—especially the sweets. Her baklava with the rose water. And of course the bougatsa…" He sighed at the memory. "The thought of you owning your own Greek bakery would make your mom *very* happy. And proud." He hesitated. "But the pregnancy thing—"

Jade patted Bunny with one hand. "Yaya always told me Mom would be over the moon at the idea of having grandchildren."

"Well, that's true. But not knowing the father…

and not *telling* the father… I don't know, honey."
He blew out another long sigh. "I'm struggling with
that myself."

There was an opportunity to deal with that now
that Trent was in town. But Jade was still afraid
of how that could change everything. What if he
wanted to try for *custody* somehow? She was nervous enough about becoming a mom, but imagining
how to navigate co-parenting with a stranger nearly
made her break out in hives.

He was here, but the thought of telling him face-
to-face made her more anxious than the idea of hitting *Send* on the email she'd written him. The email
she hadn't found the courage to send yet.

"Dad, I don't need the father's help to raise this
baby. And his life won't change if he never knows…"
It was a feeble argument. She liked her independence, but for all she knew, Trent *had* a kid and could
help with parenting.

"This isn't only about what *you* need. Your child
deserves to know her father. And the man may not
know his life has changed, but the entire trajectory
of his life will be drastically different if he never
discovers he's a father. The lost moments. The lost
memories. The lost relationship—"

"The lost court dates and custody battles." Her
voice was sharp, as much from fear as anything.
"It's more complicated than this Pollyanna image
you have in your mind. And frankly, it's my deci-

sion to make." She was clinging to what little control she had.

"I know both of those things." His voice was flat,
but not angry. "Just...*think* about it, okay?" There
was a long pause. "And I will try to get back there
to see you soon. Marla may not be able to join me,
but I have some business coming up in New York
City and could hop up there for a day."

Even if Marla were "able" to visit, she wouldn't.
Marla still hadn't forgiven Jade for the dance floor
fiasco at Ashley's wedding. Ashley, on the other
hand, had moved on from it all by the time she and
Kyle returned from their honeymoon. Turned out the
whole *Keystone Cops* chain of events had gone more
viral than any of the carefully planned moments of
her wedding day. Ashley credited Jade with helping
her gain a thousand new followers. *Glad to help, sis.*

The next day was busy. Wednesdays and Fridays
were bougatsa days, where she served up trays of
the cream-filled flaky Greek pastry. After just a few
weeks, the word had spread and the lines were growing. Joe was working in the kitchen today while Jade
manned the counter.

She was nervous that Trent would show up again,
but there'd been no sign of him by the time she was
closing up at two. Had his visit been a figment of her
imagination? Could pregnancy do that? Yesterday
had been an off day for her, with the dizzy spells

and general exhaustion. Okay, she was grasping at straws to think Trent hadn't been real, but…no one else had seen him, so…what was the harm in believing? She laughed at herself as she headed to her loft to change into running clothes.

Maybe that's what she'd been lacking yesterday—healthy exercise. She refilled her water bottle. She'd also been dehydrated yesterday. Not a good combo, and she knew better. Opening the bakery had upended her self-care schedule, and it was time to reclaim it. Her father was right—this pregnancy wasn't only about her. She had to take care of Bunny, too. Her doctor had assured her that she should be able to do whatever exercise she'd done before getting pregnant, through the second trimester as long as she didn't push herself. She'd always loved running, ever since high school. That's why she'd agreed to meet Mel Brannigan for a quick run—well…*jog*—this afternoon.

She trotted down the back stairs to the small parking lot that stretched behind the buildings that faced Main Street, and waved at Benjamin Adamu, who was renting the neighboring apartment above Asher Peyton's furniture shop.

"Running away from it all, Jade?" The graduate student jogged down the steps to his compact car. "It's so much easier to drive!"

"Oh ha ha." She rolled her eyes with a smile. She'd

heard his joke a dozen times before. "The point is to get exercise, wise guy."

He gestured to her visible baby bump under the clingy T-shirt and winked. "Looks like you've already had some exercise."

Oh, the bold sassiness of youth before they learned boundaries. She'd forgotten to zip her jacket, and it was the only thing that still hid Bunny from the world. Pretty soon even the jacket wouldn't work. Like…by next week. She shrugged at Benjamin, pointing to her belly.

"What, this? Oh, I just had a big lunch." She dropped her smile. "Don't tell anyone, okay?"

He started to laugh, then looked at her face and his eyes went wide. "Oh. Yeah. Understood. It's not like I hang out with your crowd…" She raised her eyebrows and he stammered. "I didn't mean anything about your age… I…uh…" He realized he had no way out. He reached for his car door. "You know what? Never mind. Have a nice run, neighbor lady!"

She was still chuckling about it when she met up with Mel in the small park between town and the resort. She told Mel about Benjamin noticing her pregnancy. They were doing a slow jog along the lakeshore. Mel glanced over at Jade's stomach, now covered with the zipped-up jacket, but still…definitely not flat.

"This isn't the type of town where people pry." Mel grinned. "And most people are smart enough not to ask a woman if she's pregnant, because if she's not...ouch." Mel looked over again and shrugged. "But that little Bunny of yours is definitely poppin'. Why are you working so hard to hide her?"

They stopped so Mel could retie her sneaker. "You don't *have* to answer that, of course." Mel stretched before straightening. "I'm just...curious. Is everything okay?"

Jade stared out over the cold-looking gray waters of Gallant Lake. The day was overcast, but at least it wasn't raining. "I'm a private person. The pregnancy was not planned. I'm not in denial..." *Much.* "But I tend to deal with one problem at a time. Not that she's a *problem*, but..."

"But she was a shock?"

"You have no idea. I didn't even *know* until the week my offer was accepted on the bakery. I was in the middle of this huge life change when another huge life change crashed the party." Her hand touched her stomach again. She knew she did that way too often, but it reminded her she wasn't alone in this adventure. "I didn't intend to keep her a secret. I was new in town and it felt weird to lead with 'my name's Jade and yes I'm pregnant.'" She stretched, leaning backward. "I wanted people to know me for *me*, if that makes sense."

"It does, actually." Mel smiled. "But you're excited, right?"

And terrified. "The timing is far from ideal, but

I knew right away I wanted this baby. I love her already."

Mel smiled. "I know. It was the same for me when I was pregnant. I adored both of them when they were the size of a jellybean." They started walking, then moved into a gentle jog again. Jade wouldn't be doing this comfortably much longer. Mel looked over at her. "Does the dad even know?"

"He's not…um…involved." She didn't mention that he was in town. That he'd been to the bakery. That his eyes had warmed with desire as soon as he saw her. That her skin had immediately remembered all the places he'd touched her on that one incredible night.

But he hadn't come back today. Sure, he'd left his room number, but all that meant was he was interested in a booty call. She was nothing more than a fling to him, and that's all she'd ever be. As long as she never told him about the baby.

She couldn't help wondering what kind of father he'd be, though. She could hardly judge him for that wild April night, since it was as much her idea as his. But if he only saw her as some sort of conquest—maybe one of many—then how would he feel about raising a child with her?

The two women finished their run and parted ways at the entrance to the park. Jade walked back down Main Street, stopping at the pretty white gazebo on the waterfront in the center of town. She sat on the steps for a few minutes. She unzipped her jacket, imagining herself sitting in this spot during the summer months. Gallant Lake was going to be a wonderful place to raise her daughter.

Dan Adams was walking down the sidewalk when she crossed the street to the closed bakery. She needed to check inventory and place an order for the weekend.

"Hi, Jade!" Dan, clearly off-duty in jeans and sweater, stopped at the corner entrance to the bakery. "You're still running, huh?" His voice trailed off and his cheeks went ruddy.

Dan was one of the nicest men Jade had met. Kind and funny, but with a deep strength and honor that always shone through. Mackenzie was lucky to have him. "It's okay, Dan. I just took a gentle jog in the park with Mel Brannigan. With my doctor's blessing."

Jade slid her key in the door. When she glanced back, there was another man walking up behind Dan. *Trent.* She froze, hand still on the key.

Trent looked between Jade and Dan with a frown. "Everything okay here?"

Jade's shoulders straightened. *Seriously?* They'd spent one nameless night together and he thought he had the right to go alpha white knight, coming to her rescue?

"That's none of your business," she snapped. She

wasn't the only one who'd bristled. Dan stepped between Trent and Jade.

"The lady's right. You can keep right on walking, pal."

Trent didn't move. His eyes were on Jade. More specifically, on Jade's abdomen. She'd forgotten about the unzipped jacket. At this angle, turning back from the door, her top very clearly outlined the round baby bump. Trent's brows came together, his forehead furrowed.

"Is that...? Are you...?"

Jade's eyes closed. She couldn't deny being pregnant. That didn't mean she had to tell him he was the father. She opened her eyes and saw nothing but concern in his expression. And surprise, of course. She did *not* see any hint of him doing the math. In that moment, she knew what she had to do. The only right thing for Bunny.

"Yes, I'm pregnant. And it's yours, Trent."

Once again, Jade had managed to leave Trent's brain incapable of functioning. He tried to absorb her words and what they meant and how it was even possible.

The guy who'd been standing with Jade stepped back, eyes round. "Holy...um...hey...this is a conversation I do *not* need to be in the middle of." He glanced at Trent then back to Jade. "Unless you need me to stay."

She shook her head, her lips pressed together tightly. "It's okay, Dan. Obviously, Trent and I know each other." She turned the key and pushed the door open. "And we have a lot to talk about."

The Dan guy stuck his hand out abruptly. "Dan Adams. I'm the police chief here, and Jade's a friend of the family." In other words, Trent thought, *I'm the law, so behave.*

He took Dan's hand, still feeling like he was having an out-of-body experience. "Trent Michaels. I… uh… I'm staying at the resort for a conference…" Dan didn't release his hand, clearly waiting for more. Trent kept his face as neutral and non-threatening as possible. "Jade and I met last spring and…uh…" The rest seemed fairly obvious.

There was a beat of silence before Dan stepped back. "I guess I should go. Um…" He gave Jade one last pointed look. "Text Mack and I later, okay?"

Just to let us know this guy hasn't kidnapped you.

She flashed a quick smile. "I will, but we're fine, Dan."

The police chief walked away, stopping once to give Trent a final, vaguely threatening look.

"Come in," Jade said. She locked the door again behind them, gesturing to the same table they'd sat at yesterday morning.

Yesterday, Trent had been surprised and intrigued to discover Jade was in Gallant Lake. But nowhere near as surprised as he'd been a few minutes ago, when he saw her obvious pregnancy bump. The apron must have hidden it yesterday.

"My eyes are up here." Jade's sarcasm was still intact. He met her gaze.

"It can't be mine." He blurted out the words more forcefully than he intended, but he couldn't help being skeptical. That night had been filled with vigorous lovemaking, but he distinctly remembered using condoms.

Jade's shoulder lifted and fell, amusement joining the caution in her eyes. It reminded him of how nervous she'd been yesterday when he showed up. Now he understood why.

"Well, it can't *not* be yours. You're the only man I've had sex with since January." She filled two cups of tea—something herbal for herself, Irish Breakfast for him.

"We used protection." He'd always been a careful man.

"What can I say—sometimes protection fails." She sat at the table, sliding his cup toward him. "There is no doubt in my mind that this baby is yours."

He heard his ex-wife's voice echoing in his head. *Why would I want you in Harper's life? You're a worse father than you are a husband...*

"It can't be mine." His protest was getting weaker. He added two packets of sugar to his tea, stirring it slowly. If what she was saying was true... Trent frowned. Was it possible it *wasn't* true? But she'd had no way of knowing he was coming to Gallant Lake this week. He dropped his head into his hands. This couldn't be happening. Another thought popped up, and he raised his head to stare at Jade.

"That was six months ago," Trent pointed out. "You tracked down my name. Why didn't you tell me before now? Hell, why didn't you tell me yesterday?"

She set her cup down. "Don't get testy with me. I hadn't decided whether to tell you at all."

"That's ridiculous!" That wasn't the word he wanted. "Wait…that's *awful*. Why wouldn't you tell me?"

Jade leaned forward. "I. Just. Did."

"Well, yeah, but only because you had no choice!"

"I had a choice, Trent. I could have told you it was none of your business."

"But that would have been a lie. You're saying you'd lie to me…"

He's sure been through *that* before.

"I'm saying I *could* have lied, and didn't. First you don't believe me, and now you're mad that I *didn't* lie to you." She sat back with a soft smile. "Actually, never mind. I get it. You're grasping for explanations. I was the same way this summer when I found out." Her smile faded. "But I'm not going to be your scapegoat. Get mad if you want, but not at me."

Trent scrubbed his hands down his face, willing his heart to slow down enough for him to think clearly.

"Fair enough. It's just…overwhelming. I can't believe I didn't notice yesterday." He was no expert on pregnant women, but shouldn't she be as big as a house by six months? "You're not that big. Are you sure you're six mo—"

"Oh, I'm sure. For one thing, I know the last time I had sex. It was April. With *you*." She tucked a stray piece of ebony hair behind her ear. "I'm tall, so I have room to carry a baby without showing a lot. Until now, at least." She looked down at the half-basketball-sized bump under her shirt.

Pregnancy. A baby. *His* baby. His adrenaline began to settle. Not because he wasn't still terrified, but at least he was wrapping his head around what was happening.

"You're having my baby." He didn't say it as a question, even though his mind was spinning with them.

Jade nodded. "Very good. Yes I am."

"What are we going to do?"

She straightened, coolness chilling her eyes.

"*You're* not going to do anything. *I'm* going to have a baby in January." She must have seen the confusion in his eyes. "What I'm saying is you're off the hook. I don't need or expect your help with anything. I'll raise her myself."

"The hell you will." Trent ground the words out through his clenched teeth. "If it's my child…wait… did you say *her*?" A baby girl. Visions of pink satin and lace filled his head. He was going to be the father of a little girl. A girl like Harper.

Jade's eyes narrowed on him. "Well, that was fast. You went from not believing me to threatening me."

"I didn't *threaten* you. But if this *is* my child, then I'm sure as hell going to be involved in raising her." Whether he should or not. "You know for sure it's a girl?"

She nodded, her eyes still guarded. "It's a girl. How exactly do you think you're going to be…" she made air quotes with her fingers "…*involved in raising her*? You live in Denver. I live in Gallant Lake. You're a sperm donor, Trent, not a father."

He sat back, feeling the words hit him like hammer strokes. When Cindy first threatened to leave him—when he'd *begged* her to let him remain part of Harper's future—she'd just laughed and reminded him that he was not Harper's father. One day he'd arrived home to a very empty house. No furniture. No family. She'd left, cutting him off completely from the little girl he'd come to love—knowing it was the way to hurt him the most.

And now he had a second chance. All he had to do was not screw it up. He leaned back in his chair, feeling a sense of determined calm settle over him.

"If you didn't want me involved, you wouldn't have told me." Her face paled a few shades, and she swallowed hard as he continued. "But you *have* told me, and trust me—I'm going to be involved." Jade shook her head so hard that some of her long hair broke free of her ponytail, but he didn't let her speak. "I don't want this to be a fight, but I'm an attorney and I know my parental rights."

Her eyes shimmered with unshed tears, and he felt his heart begin to soften. But none of those tears spilled over. She wasn't weakening. She was regrouping. She stood and pointed to the door.

"I'm sorry I told you she's yours."

"Jade…"

"Please go."

He left, and every step down the sidewalk sent another question through his head. Was she sorry she told him because it was a lie?

Was Jade really carrying his child? And if so, what the *hell* was he going to do about it?

Chapter Seven

Jade locked the door behind Trent, but it wasn't easy with the way her hands were shaking. To his credit, he left when she told him to, but his parting words were still rattling in her head.

"This isn't over."

Everything she'd feared had come true in the first half hour that Trent knew he was the father of her child. He wanted to be *involved*. Not just wanted, but *demanded* to be. He'd even resorted to the *I'm a lawyer* routine, as if that was supposed to scare... Jade shook her head. Who was she kidding? It *had* scared her.

Most women would *want* the father of their child to be involved in raising it. But Jade could do this alone. It was for the best, since working with others was not a strength of hers. She was the in-charge type. She'd been benched more than once in college basketball because the coach said she needed to be more of a team player.

She went into the kitchen and started a batch of brown butter cookies for tomorrow morning. As she measured out the ingredients, she felt her tension ease. She worked the batter with a wooden spoon instead of the electric beater, and the physical effort helped clear her mind. Trent had clearly been in shock—his emotions had been all over the place. She got it. She'd been the same way when she found out. Angry. Happy. Terrified.

Once he had a chance to sit and think it through, he might change his mind completely. He might see that his involvement wasn't necessary. That Jade had let him off the hook, and he should be happy. She didn't want money from him. She didn't want anything from him. He was free.

Her phone chirped in her pocket just as she was putting the last sheet of cookies in the oven. The text was from Mackenzie Adams. Jade scolded herself for forgetting to text her as promised.

M: Is Baby Daddy still there?

J: No. Tell Dan I'm fine. It's all good.

M: Do you want to talk?

J: Nope.

She realized how harsh that sounded and followed it up.

J: But thanks for offering! :)

M: Uh-huh. I'll see you in the morning, my friend. Call if you need anything.

J: Will do!

She finished up in the kitchen and headed home to shower and put her feet up. She wasn't used to having this tight circle of friends who cared so fiercely. She'd only been in Gallant Lake for a few months, and already she had a contact list full of women who would show up the instant she asked them to. Maybe it was time to stop pushing them away with her "I'm fine" routine.

The truth was—she was terrified.

She wasn't surprised when Mack showed up the next day around noon, along with Nora and Amanda. They chatted among themselves while she worked. It was their way of quietly showing their support. She delivered a plate of cookies to them.

"On the house. You ladies aren't exactly subtle, but I appreciate you being here."

Nora shrugged. "I have no idea what you mean. We're just supporting a local business."

"And the local business owner." Amanda grinned. "Nice apron."

Jade had tied her new blue apron more snugly over her knit top this morning, so Bunny was fully revealed to the world. Only a few customers had reacted, and even then, it was usually just a nod and a smile. Mrs. Hendrix from the town hall had Jade's favorite reaction, exclaiming "Oh! It's a baby!" as if she'd just discovered gold. She'd congratulated Jade, then left an extra large tip in the jar on the counter—a whole dollar instead of her usual quarter.

Jade patted Bunny, who'd been doing gentle somersaults all morning, making her laugh and feel vaguely nauseous at the same time. "Not much sense in hiding her."

"You mean now that the father-to-be knows?" Mack asked, then grimaced. "Sorry. I told them. I'm the world's worst secret-keeper."

Nora pulled out a chair and patted the seat. The shop was quiet, so Jade sat.

"About like you'd expect," she answered. "Shock. Denial. Anger. And a sudden desire to be an active father figure, which I do not need."

Nora frowned. "So he wants to be involved in Bunny's upbringing? That's a good thing, right?"

"I don't think he knows which end is up right now.

I'm not sure he even *believes* me. But… I don't *need* him being involved. I can do this myself."

If she said it often enough, maybe she'd start to believe it.

"Just because you *can* doesn't mean you *should*," Nora pointed out. "I know you like being independent, or you're just *used* to being independent, but if this guy really wants to be supportive… Wait, you dated the guy, right? He's not an ax-murderer or something awful, is he?"

"That's just it—I *didn't* date him. I don't even *know* him."

Silence fell over the front of the bakery. Joe was humming as he cleaned up in back, but that was the only sound for several long minutes.

Amanda finally cleared her throat. "I know this is none of our business. You can tell me to go to hell if you want, but…how is that possible?"

"It was a one-night stand." Jade looked up, glad not to see judgment in anyone's eyes. "An impulsive, passionate night between two adults who'd never met before. We used protection. But…surprise!" She patted Bunny.

Amanda nodded. "We were using birth control when we conceived Maddy. Just a few days off the pill when I was in the hospital, and suddenly we were expecting."

Jade's tension eased. It was nice to be with friends who not only believed her, but supported her. When she'd told Dad and Marla in September, her step-mother had accused her of intentionally getting pregnant, just to upstage Ashley by having the first grandchild. Never mind that Jade was the oldest by twelve years.

"How did he find out you were here?" Mack asked. "It's kind of romantic that he tracked you down."

"There is *nothing* romantic going on, and he didn't track me down. It was a complete fluke that we saw each other again."

Nora wasn't convinced. "You're saying that two strangers from St. Louis *coincidentally* ran into each other in little Gallant Lake, New York?"

"I never said he was from St. Louis."

"No matter where he's from, how did you both end up here at the same time?"

An older woman came through the door, and Jade stood to greet her. She looked back at the table. Time to really scandalize them. She lowered her voice dramatically.

"The baby was conceived here in Gallant Lake."

The excited gasps that rose behind her as she headed to the counter made her chuckle. Once she'd boxed up some Greek pastries for the customer, she poured herself a hot cup of tea and returned to the tables. Everyone's eyes were wide with anticipation.

"The hell with whether we *should* ask or not—spill it, girl." Mack took a cookie from the plate on the table. "All the deets, please."

Jade debated for a moment, but these women were her friends. She looked at Amanda.

"It happened at the resort."

The petite blonde looked scandalized and thrilled at the same time. "No way! How?"

She told them the whole story, ignoring their wide-eyed expressions. There was one last collective gasp of delight, then they sighed in unison.

"That *screams* romance," Amanda insisted. "A sexy no-name tryst between two strangers seeking solace in each other's arms for one night? That sounds straight out of one of those romance novels in the grocery store—hot hot *hot*!"

That night was hot, alright. That night changed her life, and not just because she conceived Bunny. Having a man listen to her, comfort her, and yes, ignite her...she'd never experienced a night like that before.

"But that still doesn't explain how he found you this week in Gallant Lake," Nora said.

"That was a total fluke. He's here for some conference at the resort and walked into the bakery Tuesday morning. He didn't notice Bunny, and we were both sort of in shock. Then he came back yesterday, and...now he knows."

"Okay, first," Mack said, "I have to say again how much I love that you call the baby *Bunny*. Every time you say it my heart just melts. And second, are you saying he *didn't* know you were pregnant, and still came back to see you yesterday? That sounds like he's interested in…more."

Jade gave a soft laugh. "More *sex* maybe. That's all we shared." She knew that wasn't quite true. "He gave me his room number on Tuesday, but I'm sure that interest evaporated once he realized I was pregnant."

"Maybe. But you're going to become parents together, and you have chemistry, so…"

Jade chewed the inside of her lip. "We're not doing anything *together*. I'm raising this child, not him."

There was a beat of silence before Nora spoke. "Honey, don't you think he has a right to have a relationship with his own child?" She gave Jade a pointed look. "What are you afraid of?"

That was a really good question. She stared at the table, trying to work out the answer in her head.

"I think I'm afraid of the unknown." She looked up. "I don't want to be tied to some random stranger for the rest of my life because of one night together. What if he wants to… I don't know…share custody or something? He lives in *Denver*. How will that work? He made a point of reminding me that he's an attorney, like he was trying to intimidate me—"

She realized the women weren't listening to her anymore. They were looking past her, to the door. She'd never even heard the bell ring. She turned to see Trent, looking at her with eyes that were surprisingly gentle.

"That was a stupid thing to say," he started, his voice low and sincere. "And I'm sorry for saying it. I don't know how *any* of this is going to work, Jade. But you're right—if this baby is mine, that one night *is* going to tie us together for the rest of our lives. So maybe we should get past the *random stranger* phase before we worry about anything else." He looked at the women at the tables and gave a lighthearted wave. "Hi, ladies. I'm Trent Michaels. The one-night stand guy."

Jade sat in stunned silence as he stepped forward to shake hands as her friends—her *so-called* friends—introduced themselves to him. What was he up to? He finally turned back to her.

"Gotta minute?"

She nodded and stood, following him to the opposite side of the shop. She ignored the whispered tittering at the table behind her. Instead, she glared at him.

"You don't need to be meeting my friends. You're *not* part of my life—"

"If you're having my daughter, you should get used to me being around…" She bristled, but he hurried ahead. "I didn't mean that to sound so caveman-ish. I spent all night trying to face reality, and this—" he gestured between them, circling his hand in the air around her baby bump "—is reality. I was thinking we should get to know each other. As more than just…"

"Booty call partners?" she offered helpfully. He grinned in response.

"Definitely more than that." He paused, rubbing the back of his neck. "Jade, will you have dinner with me at the resort tonight? Let's see if we can approach this situation as friends, okay?" His gold eyes were still kind, and she felt her resolve weakening. She'd framed him as some sort of rival—a thief come to steal something from her—but that wasn't fair. He deserved the chance to show otherwise. If he was serious about being in Bunny's life, she was going to be seeing Trent Michaels for *years*. Birthdays. Graduation. Wedding. Grandchildren. She shuddered. Her life was no longer her own. She was going to have a daughter. And… She looked at Trent. A man in her life. *This* man.

"Okay." She glanced at the clock—almost closing time. "I tend to eat early these days. I have to be up around four thirty every morning to get things cooking in the bakery."

Trent frowned. "Those are long hours for someone in your condition. Can't you let your staff do the—"

"My *staff*?" She laughed. "My *staff* consists of one retired baker and me." She shook her head at Trent. "Just to be clear, you and I may end up being co-parents, but you will have *no* say in how I run my business or live my life. Got it?"

He held up both hands. "Got it. Your business is

not my business. But just to be *clear*, I was only asking out of concern."

"My doctor supports everything I'm doing." Dr. Madison was actually a little worried about her long hours on her feet. But she was fine. *Fine.*

Trent looked beyond her to her friends. "Is she always this contrary, ladies?"

They laughed, and Nora answered. "We've only known her a few months, but…yes."

"Thanks a lot." Jade couldn't help laughing, too. She looked back to Trent. "Is five o'clock okay for dinner?"

He started to nod, then looked up to the ceiling and grimaced. "I just remembered I don't have a car. It's not very chivalrous, but…meet me at the resort?"

"That works."

She didn't want to like the guy. But as he headed out the door with another wave, she realized it wouldn't be good to *not* like the guy, either. Not if he was going to be in her life forever. It couldn't hurt to get to know each other and at least be *friendly*, if not exactly friends.

Trent changed his tie twice, then threw the third one on the bed and took off his dress shirt. Too formal. He pulled a sweater from the closet and stared at it. Too casual? He muttered a curse under his breath. Why was he so damn nervous? This wasn't a job interview. He snorted. If Jade was right, he already *had* the job of being a dad-to-be. So why was he nervous tonight? He tugged the dark red sweater over his head and looked in the mirror.

He was nervous because he wanted to impress Jade. His mouth twisted. *Impress* wasn't the right word. He wanted her to *like* him. Practically speaking, everything would be easier if she did. He stared at the mirror. She still had the ability to make his skin tingle just from being near her. That had happened when they met in April, too. It was as if she radiated a special energy just for him.

But tonight wasn't a date. For one thing, she was six months pregnant, although it didn't do a thing to make him less attracted to her. But they barely knew each other. And they had to determine how they were going to…how had she put it? Co-parent.

Holy hell.

He sat on the edge of the bed. Was he really going to be a father? If so, his life's trajectory had just changed *forever*. He was having a daughter. A little girl. Ballet lessons. Barbie dolls. Or maybe she'd like Tonka trucks and hockey. He didn't care.

The question was—what kind of father could he possibly be? He'd tried once, with Harper, and Cindy had taken her away from him without a second thought. Would Jade try to keep him away from their daughter? He chewed his lip. He'd fight that, of course, but it would be easier if they could figure this out together. Over dinner.

One of the first things they needed—*he* needed—to figure out was if he should believe her. Jade was so bluntly direct that she seemed incapable of not telling the truth. But he'd thought Cindy was honest, too.

He stared out the window to the lake and the surrounding mountains. Yeah, he had trust issues. With other people, but most of all with himself. He had a hard time trusting his own judgment *about* other people. So how could he trust himself to be capable of raising a *child*?

His own laughter echoed in the silent room. He'd thought his biggest challenge this week was going to be making a decision on a career change. Now here he was, trying to figure out what kind of *father* he was going to be. His own father hadn't exactly been a shining example to follow. But he was getting ahead of himself. First—get to know the woman who was giving birth to his daughter.

He'd only been at the table five minutes when she came breezing into the restaurant. The dinner crowd was thin this early, but she turned every head in the place.

She strode across the room, her dark hair long and free around her shoulders. He hadn't seen her hair free like that since they were in his hotel room together six months ago. He liked it. She was wearing flats instead of the heels she'd worn that night. She wore black leggings under a long, fluttery loose-knit sweater of soft cinnamon brown. A colorful scarf of fall colors completed the look—she was an autumn wood nymph. Graceful and…very obviously pregnant. The soft sweater hugged her baby bump.

He was so mesmerized by the sight of her that he ended up scrambling to his feet just before she got to the table, wondering what to do next. Hug her? Kiss her? Maybe a peck on the cheek? Shake her hand?

She stopped when she realized how confused he was. Apparently she didn't have an answer either. They'd been as intimate as two people could be. They'd created new *life* together. And yet, they were basically strangers. Her mouth slanted into that snarky grin that he was beginning to realize was a signature look for her.

"Why don't you start by pulling out a chair for me, Romeo."

He pulled a chair out, then surprised both of them by leaning over after she sat to brush his lips against her hair. She smelled like sugar and musk and it immediately brought back memories of their night together.

"You look amazing, my Juliet." He whispered the words, his heart pounding so hard he feared she might hear it. He straightened abruptly, then chuckled. "Why do I feel like an awkward high school sophomore on his first date?"

She smiled, snark-free, as he sat. "It is a little surreal. We're running this relationship backwards—sex first, then our first date six months later." Her cheeks went pink. "Well, maybe not *date*, but…whatever this is." She gestured over the table between them. "A friendly dinner. Then again, we're not really *friends* either, so… I don't know what the hell we're doing. A business meeting?"

She was as nervous as he was, which helped Trent relax. He shook his head. "Let's not call it business. We may have arrangements to discuss, but not tonight. I think a friendly dinner works for us. It's fair to say we *like* each other, or this—" he gestured at her stomach "—wouldn't have happened."

"I call *this*—" she copied his hand gesture at her stomach "—Bunny."

"Bunny?" He had no idea what she was talking about.

Her cheeks reddened again. "When I first found out, I didn't know if it was a girl or boy and wasn't sure I wanted to. But I didn't want to refer to her as *it*, so… Bunny." She gave a tiny shrug. "You know… bun in the oven? Perfect for a baker, right? After I found out it was a girl, the name stuck. I mean, not *forever*, but I don't know if I can give her a permanent name before I meet her, so… Bunny." She patted the baby bump. *His* baby bump. Or at least, his baby.

"Bunny," he repeated. "Okay." The server took their order—steak and dark beer for him, broiled salmon and sparkling water for Jade. It was time to get started on this Getting To Know You mission. "So… St. Louis. Is that where you grew up?"

She took a sip of water. "Diving right in, eh? St. Louis became home when I was ten and my father married Marla. Before that, I lived with my mom in Berwyn, which is right outside Chicago. There's a pretty big Greek community there."

"Gee, you mean Marla's not your birth mom?" He winked. The petite, puffy-haired blonde looked *nothing* like Jade. It was no surprise she had Mediterranean heritage with her dark hair and complexion.

Jade huffed a short laugh at his joke. "Hardly. My *real* mom was beautiful, inside and out. She met my dad at college, and they fell in love. Dad was in a big-shot financial firm and we had one of a thousand brick bungalows in Berwyn. Life was like the movie *My Big Fat Greek Wedding*, and I loved it." Her expression fell. "I was eight when Mom died in a car accident." She paused. "Dad met Marla and the next thing I knew, we were moving to St. Louis."

Their shrimp cocktails arrived, and Trent smiled when Jade grabbed a giant shrimp and scooped up half a cup of cocktail sauce before popping it into her mouth. She looked over at him and her eyes narrowed. "What?"

"Nothing." He grinned at her. "I like seeing a woman enjoy her food."

"Are you seriously commenting on a pregnant woman's appetite?"

"Uh…no." He straightened. "Definitely not." He

cleared his throat. "Life in St. Louis wasn't great, then?"

"It was okay." She looked up, her eyes darker than ever. "It wasn't all bad. I don't think Marla knew what to do with me. I was tall and loud and into sports. Marla was...not any of those things. Ashley came along two years later, a perfect little reflection of Marla. To be fair, I was no prize. I came into her life as a gangly, resentful preteen."

"But *Marla* was the adult. She should have been prepared for that."

Jade seemed surprised when he jumped to her defense.

"Whatever." She brushed it off. "I came into her life just as I was learning that I didn't fit in."

"In the family?"

"Anywhere." She ate her last shrimp, then sat back as the server exchanged appetizers for the main dishes. Her flat-toned response didn't compute for him.

"What do you mean, *anywhere*?" he asked. "You're smart, beautiful..."

She held up a hand. "I was neither of those things in my teens, and please stop buttering me up. You already went all the way with me, remember?"

Trent leaned forward. "First, I'm not buttering you up. And second... I definitely remember. That was a night I'll *never* forget."

She snorted. "Neither of us will." She patted her baby bump.

He felt a flash of annoyance. "I'm not talking about… Bunny. I'm talking about that night. It was incredible—one of a kind, Jade. Wasn't it the same for you?"

The question might sound needy, but she didn't seem to take it that way. She set her fork down and looked straight into his eyes.

"It really was an incredible night. But don't you think a lot of that had to do with the circumstances? A full moon glistening on the water. A bottle of wine. Neither of us wanting to be at that wedding."

"A pulverized stiletto?"

Her laughter bubbled up. The sound of it—all whiskey-tinged and bright—sent a jolt of electricity through his bloodstream. He wondered what she'd say if he told her he'd kept the remaining shoe, tucking it into his pocket and bringing it home with him.

"Oh my God, my poor shoe! And the way you sent it flying into the lake…" She kept laughing, wiping the corner of her eye. "Why didn't you run as soon as you came across my crazy-town moment?"

"I liked your crazy-town. Your meltdown was magnificent." He hesitated. "*You* were magnificent."

Her eyes went wide as saucers, but she didn't argue. They finished eating in silence. The server was clearing their plates when Jade's mouth tilted into her classic bemused grin.

"I feel like I'm being interviewed here, and I already *have* the job. So what's *your* life story? Has Denver always been home?"

He *had* been grilling her a bit, even if it was out of genuine curiosity. They shared a slice of the restaurant's famous lava cake in a spun sugar cage while he filled her in on his childhood in Denver. Cold, detached father. Loving, but equally detached mother. Their divorce when he was fourteen. Law school—the only option if his dad was paying. A dream of saving the planet, and the reality of following his *father's* dream for him—sensible corporate law. The same firm that sent him to a wedding in April.

"And *that's* the tenuous thread that brought us together," Jade said with a tight smile. "Two tragic childhoods joined by the thinnest of connections. And, of course, a child of our own. What could possibly go wrong with this picture?"

"My childhood wasn't tragic. Just…lonely." He shrugged. "I was incredibly privileged." He ran his fingers through his hair. "My parents loved me the best they could." Unfortunately, that love always felt conditional.

Jade nodded, tracing her finger around the top of her coffee cup. "I feel the same way about my dad. He had a new wife and a brand-new daughter. He needed me to step up and be the big sister." The corner of her mouth lifted. "I did my best, but I was always the odd one out."

His head tipped to the side. "You keep saying that. You said something like that the night of the wedding. That you didn't fit in. What does that mean, exactly?"

"You remember that?" She looked at him from under her long, black eyelashes.

"Honey, I remember *everything* about that night."

Her brows gathered together. "I am *not* your honey."

"I didn't mean it like…" He winced. "Okay. It sounded bad. Sorry. But I do remember every second of the time we spent together, Jade. So tell me, why don't you think you fit in?"

Her smile faltered. "Look at me. I'm six feet tall. I'm loud and sarcastic and I could care less what people think about that. I *played* sports instead of just cheerleading them. My stepmom and sister are pretty little blondes and I'm…not. I've just always been the weird one, you know?"

Before he thought about what he was doing, he reached forward and covered her hand with his. Just like any other time he came in contact with her, his pulse jumped.

"Being strong, smart and gorgeous doesn't make you weird, Jade."

She gave a snort of laughter. *"Gorgeous?"* She nodded toward his beer. "How many of those have you had?"

"You know I've only had one." He gave her hand

a squeeze. "And you *are* gorgeous. Even more than before. You're…"

"I swear to God, Trent—" she was laughing and stopped to catch her breath "—if you say I'm *glowing*, I will hurt you."

Oh yeah—he definitely liked the sound of her laughter. It was strong and edgy and deep. He liked her sassy attitude. He liked *her*.

He watched as she wiped a bit of chocolate from the corner of her mouth with her finger. A chill ran across his skin as he thought about her words. *I will hurt you.*

She'd been kidding, but the truth was—Jade Malone could hurt him in so many ways.

Chapter Eight

Jade had no idea why her hand was still in Trent's. She could pull away. She *should*. But she didn't. Even when he was giving her that big grin after she'd just threatened him with bodily harm.

"I'm serious," she said, finally reining in her laughter. "It's like it's the only thing people can say to pregnant women. I'm not *glowing*, I'm sweating. I'm exhausted. My feet swell like balloons by the end of the day. And—" A wave of unexpected emotion washed over her. "And I have no idea how I'm going to do this." Her voice cracked.

"Hey…" He leaned forward, his voice low and soft. "You're not in this alone. That's why we're here tonight, remember?"

"I don't know *why* I'm here tonight," she snapped.

That wasn't fair. She took a breath and met his gaze. "I'm sorry. I know we're…um…getting to know each other. I'm just…" She took a deep breath, then laughed. "I guess I *am* glowing with something— hormones and emotions. Sorry. It comes out of no- where sometimes." She didn't like surprises. She especially didn't like surprises coming out of her tear ducts when the hormones kicked in.

"I meant what I said." Trent gazed deep into her eyes. "We're in this together."

Jade blinked. She wasn't used to people being on her side like this. Especially a near-stranger. Trent made her feel like he meant it. She stared at their two hands together, then turned hers to wind her fingers into his. He didn't move at first, then his fingers tightened. The extra connection made something in her chest ease. She wasn't alone. She looked up and met his eyes, now more like chocolate than whis- key. Dark, warm and inviting. Jade sat up straight.

No no no. She could *not* see any invitation in those eyes. Her life was complicated enough. She gently pulled her hand from his.

"Why are you still single?" She blurted the thought out loud. How was a good-looking attorney like Trent not taken?

He gave a soft laugh. "I could ask you the same question. But I'm not *still* single. I'm single again. Divorced." His smile remained, but there was a tightness around his eyes that told her this was not a happy topic. "You?"

She shook her head. "A restaurant pastry chef's life isn't easy on relationships—lots of long, late hours. A few relationships came and inevitably went." She'd just never found the right fit, and finally decided that guy might not exist for her. "Speaking of long hours, I really do need to go. It's not late for normal people, but when you're pregnant *and* a baker…"

Trent moved quickly to his feet to pull her chair out. "I understand. No problem. Let me walk you out." He tossed a tip on the table and nodded to the server when she asked if he wanted it charged to his room.

"That's not necessary." She knew she sounded prickly, but she didn't think it was a good idea to remain in close proximity to this man, who, for some reason, felt like maybe he could be a perfect fit for her. But that couldn't be true. Had to be the hormones.

Trent let her lead the way, but stayed with her. "I let you be the independent woman driving here on your own. I forced myself to sit in here and wait instead of being a gentleman and meeting you at the door." His hand brushed the small of her back as they walked to the entrance. "I am damn sure not going to let you walk to your car in the dark."

"Afraid your gentleman card will be permanently revoked?"

He chuckled. "It could happen."

They crossed the lobby, and he held open the door. It *was* dark outside. She glanced at her watch and groaned. Had they really talked for two hours?

"No wonder I flipped the emotion switch. I didn't know it was seven o'clock already. Time flew by."

"Are you okay to drive home?"

"It's only three miles. And downhill all the way. I think I'll be fine."

"Just a reminder that I have no idea where you live."

"Oh…yeah. Right." He was only in town through the weekend. What difference did it make if he knew where she lived? "I'm renting a loft in town, just a few doors from the bakery. It's above the coffee shop."

Trent frowned. "A loft? I get that it's close to work, but…isn't that a lot of steps for you when you're…"

"I'm pregnant, not terminally ill." She rolled her eyes. "Women have babies all the time, you know."

"Yeah, yeah, I know. But it's never been someone having *my* baby."

She stopped abruptly. "You mean the baby *I'm* carrying and raising?" Agitation pulsed under her skin, and tears threatened to spill over again. Everyone kept telling her she wasn't doing this alone, but she *was*. She'd lived her entire life that way—alone. "Just because you're the biological father, that doesn't mean you get to tell me where or how to live, or how to raise this child."

"Damn it, Jade." He scrubbed the back of his neck, staring up at the parking lot light. "I can't tell if this is hormones flaring again, or if you actually think I'm not going to have a voice in my own daughter's upbringing. Tonight was about getting to know each other, but if you want to start laying out legal and financial arrangements for how we're going to co-parent, then we can do that." He gave her a pointed look. "If that's my child, I'm going to be an active parent in her life."

Jade blinked a few times, holding the tears back by sheer will. "First, don't ever tell me or any woman what you think about their hormones. Not ever. Not unless you're cruising for a black eye." She waved her finger in his face, almost smiling when he leaned back. "And second, let me assure you that I *will* dictate how things are done while I'm carrying this baby. As long as she's in *my* body, you have nothing to say about it." She pressed her key fob to unlock her little red car. "And if you *still* don't believe she's yours, we'll do a DNA test after she's born. I have no problem with that." Her hand slid over Bunny, her protective instincts in high gear. "She's yours, Trent." Her voice cracked, and she pressed her lips together in frustration. Her hand shook when she opened the car door and slid in.

Trent put out his hand to prevent the door from

closing and knelt at her side. "This isn't how I want tonight to end." His brows knit together. "When I tell you I want to be involved, it doesn't mean I'm going to dictate anything. Yes, if I'm her father, I want to be in her life." He reached over and took her hand. Once again, she didn't pull away from his hold. He looked down to the ground, almost talking to himself. "I don't want you thinking of me as some baby-stealing monster." He paused, then looked up at her, his eyes soft. "Remember—you've had six months to get used to this news. I've had two days. But we do have more talking to do."

It had been a long day, and her alarm would be going off at four thirty in the morning. The thought made her sag in her seat. She patted Trent's hand before pulling her other hand free.

"You've got a point—this is brand new to you." She needed time to put her *own* thoughts in order, and Trent probably needed that even more than she did. "Aren't you here for a convention or something?"

"Well, yeah." He tipped his head and winked at her. *Whoa.* His wink was as sexy as the rest of him. "But I think this…uh…situation…is a lot more important."

"I just…" She closed her eyes and sighed. She was exhausted, physically and emotionally. "I planned on doing inventory tomorrow after we close, and on Saturday I'm baking for a big event—" She looked at him and laughed softly. "—A big event here at the resort. I'm guessing it's for the conference. My point is…maybe we should both take a minute. I'm not saying go away…"

"Just go away for now, right? I get it." He sat back on his heels, then rose to his feet when she yawned. "You should get home and get some rest. And that's a suggestion, not a command." He was studying her, as if trying to figure her out like a puzzle. *Good luck with that.* "Tell you what—I have workshops I want to attend tomorrow, and I'm going for a climb on Saturday, but things wrap up here by midday Sunday. Can I stop by and talk to you after that? That should give us both time to be able to think and plan more rationally."

Right before he left town? That would be perfect for everyone.

"Okay. If the bakery is closed, you can come up to my apartment. It's number 2D. There's an entrance in back, just use the fire escape stairs."

"I'll call before I head over… I guess we should exchange numbers?"

There was no point in refusing. They exchanged numbers, and he tapped on the hood of her car as she backed out of the parking spot. Despite her occasional waves of panic about his unexpected presence, Trent seemed to be trying *not* to appear threatening in any way. But she didn't know the man and had no idea what was genuine and what was an act. He was an attorney, which meant he was probably a skilled negotiator…or manipulator.

Jade had relied on her healthy skepticism and general mistrust of others for years. Her *outsider syndrome* had created a barrier that anyone in her life had to climb over before they became part of her small, trusted circle of friends. She made the short drive home and headed up the metal stairs to her apartment. She'd made mistakes before. Every mistake made that barrier higher.

She wasn't just protecting herself now. She was protecting Bunny, too. As if reading her mind, the baby did a little roll, creating a fluttering movement that felt like a bubble popping underwater. Little ripples of motion inside of her. New life.

Jade felt her heart swell with emotion. She was strong enough to carry this child, and she was strong enough to protect her. Trent was the father, but Jade still planned on keeping her skepticism solidly in place. Even if the man did manage to make her barriers tremble every time he touched her.

"You actually suggested to her face that she was hormonal?" Nick West started to laugh, leaning back on his hands as they sat on top of the Shawangunk cliffs, several thousand feet above the valley below. "Man, you're old enough to know better. You're lucky she didn't slap you right then and there."

Everyone he'd met in this town seemed to know

Jade was carrying his child, and they all seemed very invested in the story. During the morning climb—which was more challenging than he'd expected—Trent had talked about his evening with Jade on Thursday. None of her personal story, of course, but how they'd talked over dinner and things seemed to be getting along fine, until she got emotional out of the blue.

"But *she* was the one who brought up her hormones in the first place!" He straightened his legs and stretched, thankful for the Saturday sunshine breaking some of the chill from the sharp wind at the top of the cliff.

"Women can talk about their hormones," Nick said. "Men cannot. That's a well-known rule of relationships. Have you never been in a relationship before?"

"Never with a pregnant woman, no." He looked out over the Catskill Mountains and the valley below. The sky was that crisp, brilliant blue of autumn. The trees were losing their foliage, but there were enough evergreens to give the landscape a color other than brown. He blew out a long breath. "I was married a few years back, but it didn't last." That divorce had broken his heart, and given him serious doubts about his ability to be a father.

"Because you asked her if she was hormonal?" Nick grinned, and Trent started to laugh.

"I don't think I ever did that. I found lots of other ways to screw up. At least according to my ex-wife."

"No children with her, I assume?"

Trent shook his head, ignoring the sharp stab in his chest. Cindy had had a daughter, and he'd loved Harper like his own, but that didn't matter to Cindy.

"Kids change everything, man." Nick reached into his small pack and handed Trent a bottle of water. "It's been less than a year, and my baby boy has turned our lives upside down. In the best ways, of course, but it's different." He glanced at Trent. "How are you going to handle living in Denver with Jade and the baby here?"

That was a really good question, and Trent didn't have an answer. "No clue. I'm still adjusting to the news, so I haven't thought that far ahead yet."

"Let me know if there's anything I can do to help. When I arrived here from LA I thought I'd landed on another planet. But there are some great folks in this town, and they are *fierce* about taking care of each other." He rose to his feet. "We should head down before this wind picks up anymore."

Trent thought about the women he'd met at the bakery, and how they'd sized him up the moment he'd walked in. They were ready to protect Jade. That was great. Except *he* wanted to be the one protecting her. Hard to do that from Colorado.

The two men prepared their lines and began the tricky descent. Nick warned Trent that he was taking a more difficult route down, and he wasn't kidding. By the time they got back to Nick's SUV, it was almost noon. Nick had agreed to drive Trent to nearby Kingston to pick up a rental car. He'd originally figured he'd be spending all his time at the conference, but being without a vehicle was chafing at him now. And since his boss had asked him to visit that client in Albany, he could charge the rental to the firm.

He'd already made arrangements with the other partners to spend more time in Gallant Lake. He'd used the Albany client as his excuse, saying he couldn't meet with them until Tuesday. Which was only because he hadn't *called* the client until yesterday morning.

Jade wasn't the only thing making him extend his stay. The conference had been stimulating and informative so far, and he was more tempted than ever to make the jump to doing what he'd always wanted. He was ready to explore his options in the northeast—closer to his new family-to-be.

On Sunday, he had lunch with Vince Grassman and Blake Randall. He told them he was hanging around for a while longer, and Vince offered to set up some meetings for him. Blake just smiled. Afterward, Trent texted Jade. It hadn't been easy to wait, but he'd needed that extra time more than he realized.

T: I'm heading down—you at the bakery?

There was a long pause before he finally saw the floating bubbles indicating she was typing.

J: Bakery's closed. I'll be at home.

T: Need anything while I'm out?

Another long pause. Had that question been too familiar? He was just putting the black Land Rover in gear to leave when her reply came through.

J: I'd kill for some good kettle chips. I'm craving them.

He smiled.

T: You got it. See you in a bit.

He pulled the Land Rover into the parking lot behind the bakery. The lot stretched behind the businesses on this side of Main Street. Most of the buildings were three stories, with businesses on the first floor and residences above. The whole stretch was laced together with metal fire escapes on the second and third stories. It was a pretty extensive system of walkways and stairs, but it did provide easy access to the apartments.

He scowled at how long and steep the first flight of stairs was, then reminded himself that Jade did not want to hear his opinions on how safe it was for her to be going up and down them. He knocked on the door and she opened it more quickly than he expected.

He held up two bags of kettle chips. "I come bearing gi—"

She snatched the bags from his hand before he could finish. "Thank God. I swear my craving got even worse once I asked you to bring them." She stepped aside so he could come in.

"Is that why you were skulking at the door?"

"I was doing laundry," she answered, nodding at the small laundry and storage room by the entrance. She opened a bag as she walked. She popped a handful of chips in her mouth and sighed as she chewed. "Oh, wow. So good."

Trent followed her into the wide open living space. The kitchen was small, but efficient and upscale, with marble counters and sleek stainless steel barstools at the island. The wall facing Main Street and the lake beyond it had two stories of windows. There were black metal stairs—so many steep, metal staircases in this building—leading to a loft bordered with industrial metal railings. He could see a glimpse of a gossamer drape coming from the ceiling to surround a tall white iron headboard.

"You sleep all the way up there?" He blurted out the question without thinking, but Jade was too busy munching potato chips to get offended.

"Yup. It's like sleeping in a tree house." She opened

the refrigerator. "Something to drink? I have water, soda and a few bottles of beer." His brow rose, and she laughed. "Not for me. My landlords, Nora and Asher Peyton, came up for dinner last week, and I bought a six-pack."

"A beer sounds good. You said they own the coffee shop downstairs?"

"Technically, the Gallant Brew is Nora's. Asher owns the furniture studio next door." She pointed to the brick wall behind Trent. "There's an apartment above that, too. They were originally neighbors who hated each other...until they fell in love and got married."

"Where do they live now?" He took the beer bottle from Jade and twisted off the top.

She looked good today—not as tired and pale as she'd been by the end of the night before. And the chips had put a smile on her face. Her hair was pulled into a low ponytail, and her soft yellow sweater showed her baby bump prominently. She took a bottle of sparkling water for herself, then went into the living area to curl up in the oversized armchair near the windows.

"Asher is also an architect, and he built an amazing log home up on Gallant Mountain. They had me up there for their annual cookout back on Labor Day." She looked around and smiled. "This was fully furnished, and I can walk to work. But I know I'll need something more practical eventually. Right now all my own furniture is in storage."

He took a seat on the sofa across from her. "As nice as this place is, it's not exactly childproof." He glanced up at the loft, with the huge space between the horizontal metal railings.

Jade ate another handful of chips, then shook her head sadly and folded the bag closed. "If I have any more of these salty, miraculous, wonderful things, my feet will be balloons tonight." She followed his gaze to the loft. "Yeah, that's a problem. But Asher said he'd put a Plexiglas liner inside the loft railing to keep Bunny from crawling through it. And a baby gate at the top of the stairs. But she won't be crawling around much until next summer. I have time."

Once again, the residents of Gallant Lake were stepping up.

"What are you going to do with the bakery for the next six months or so?"

Her eyes narrowed dangerously. It was always a little scary when she did that. "What are you talking about?"

"You'll be on maternity leave soon. It's almost November. You said you're due in January. And after you have her, you'll need to be home with her…"

The anger faded from her eyes, but it was replaced with something more annoying. She was amused.

"I'm not a fragile flower, Trent. Being pregnant doesn't make me incapable of doing my job." She shifted in the chair, tucking her feet farther underneath her. She was definitely still flexible. "I only expect to stay home for a month or so after she's born. I'll probably bring her with me to the bakery in the early mornings, and have someone babysit during normal hours." She chuckled. "Hard to convince anyone to start babysitting at four thirty in the morning."

"You're only taking a *month* for maternity leave?" Trent sat up straight. "That doesn't sound like much."

She stared at him for a minute, then shook her head. "I can't just close the doors because I'm having a baby. And don't forget, the bakery closes at two, so I'll have plenty of time with her every afternoon."

He frowned. "I suspect your work isn't done just because the shop closes. You have bookkeeping and baking and cleanup to do, right?"

"Joe has agreed to work full-time until at least May, which takes a lot of pressure off of me. If I need time away, I'll take it." Her eyebrows lowered. "You *do* remember I don't need your approval for any of this, right?"

He scrubbed his hands down his face and let out a heavy sigh. "I just… I can't help worrying, okay? And me asking a few questions doesn't mean I disapprove. I want to help, Jade."

"Don't need your help." Her answer was sharp. A little *too* sharp. Was she trying to convince him or herself?

"Have you always been this difficult about accepting help?"

Her eyes went wide. He thought she might be angry, but instead she started to laugh.

"As a matter of fact, yes. Some people have even suggested I'm a control freak, but I think I just know the best ways to do things in my own life. The best for *me*." Her smile faded. "I've had to rely on myself for a long time, Trent. I'm not inclined to take advice from a stranger."

"Calling me a stranger is a bit of a stretch when you're carrying my child."

"So you finally believe the baby is yours? No more ifs?"

She'd offered to take a DNA test without hesitation, and he couldn't come up with any serious reason to doubt her.

"I believe you. We're about to become parents together."

She snorted. "Don't get carried away with the *together* stuff." There was that sharpness again. She was so defensive.

"Jade, I'm just trying to figure out my role here. I'm trying to decide what to do next."

The corner of Jade's mouth slanted upward, but her eyes were cool. "I can answer that for you. Go back to Denver, and…don't do anything. Simply live your life, Trent. You don't need to have any role here at all."

She was working awfully hard to push him away. He stared at the floor, resting his elbows on his knees. "And what would you think of me if I did that? What would you think of me if I left tomorrow morning and never looked back?" She started to answer, but he held up his hand to make her wait. "I'm not asking how *you* would feel if I did what you've asked me to do. I'm asking what would you think about *me* if I did it. What kind of man would I be in your eyes? If you heard that someone you cared about did that—just abdicated responsibility for his child—what would you say to him?"

Chapter Nine

Jade wanted to say his questions were pointless. His unexpected appearance in Gallant Lake had forced her hand on telling him about the baby, but she'd made it clear she didn't want or expect anything from him.

But he'd struck a nerve. Sure, she could handle this on her own. Watching Trent walk away would remove a complication from her life. But it wasn't that simple.

Silence fell over the apartment, broken only by the sound of an occasional car going by on the street below. She could hear her father's voice saying *this isn't about just you anymore.* She unfolded her legs from under herself and leaned forward, matching Trent's pose and looking him straight in the eyes.

"I *want* you to leave—" She shook her head when

he tried to speak. She needed to talk this out. "No, let me finish. In some ways it would be more convenient for *me* if you left. I'm very good at relying on myself to do things. But you're right. I'd think less of you if you did. Maybe not right away. But eventually... I would think less of you as a person. As a father." She chewed her lower lip. "I hadn't thought it through all the way to that point before now."

Even when he'd kept insisting he intended to be involved, she'd held on to the hope that he'd just... go away. That he'd panic and run. That he'd decide a baby didn't fit in his tidy lifestyle. Decide she was capable of doing this on her own after all. Decide he didn't want to be tied to her forever if they seriously attempted co-parenting. Lots of people had decided it was easier not to be tied to her—her stepmom, her former employer, a few boyfriends.

But Dad had been right. Those hopes to go it alone were selfish. It wasn't fair to Trent or to their daughter. She was asking him to be less of a man. She cleared her throat carefully, getting ready to say two sentences she rarely uttered out loud.

"I'm sorry. I was wrong." She sat up straight. "If you want to be in her life, then I guess we really do have to figure out a future...together." She gave herself a shake, trying to erase the illogical shot of pleasure that thought brought. "I mean, not *together*-together. But as parents together. I have no idea how that's going to work when you live on the opposite side of the country."

His expression softened. "They have these new-fangled things called airplanes, and using them means Denver is a four-hour flight away."

"Just understand you'll be the one making that trip for a lot of years. I'm not putting our little girl on a plane alone."

Our little girl... Sometimes when she said things like that out loud it really hit her—she was going to have a little girl. She was going to be a mom. She swallowed the panic that rose up.

Trent's face twisted. "I wouldn't want that, either. I've been needing to make some big decisions for a while now. Maybe this is the kick in the butt I needed."

"What kind of decisions?" He'd said he wasn't in a relationship, but... "Is there a woman back home you need to explain this to?"

He shook his head. "Nothing like that, no. I haven't been in a serious relationship since my divorce two years ago."

"What happened to the marriage?"

There was a long beat of silence before he answered.

"Lots of things happened."

She waited, but he didn't expand on his answer. There was a story there, but he wasn't telling. He looked up. "How about you? I know you said I was the only one who *could* be the father, but…was there someone else in your life before…um… Bunny?"

"No. No one recent, anyway." She shrugged. "Like I said the other night, my work hours weren't conducive to a healthy dating life."

"Because you get up so early? That doesn't seem—"

"I was a pastry chef at an upscale restaurant in St. Louis. Mornings weren't the problem. It was the nights that were always booked. The only people I saw were other cooks and servers in a noisy, high-pressure kitchen. Add that to my height challenge, and…"

"Supermodels are tall, and people don't mind dating them."

Jade rolled her eyes. "You'd be surprised. Men's egos are incredibly fragile. Even when someone shorter *did* date me, they almost always asked me to wear flat shoes around them. That always ticked me off. Why shouldn't I wear whatever I want to wear?"

"Agreed. I'm guessing you're what…six-one?"

She nodded. "Just don't ask me how the weather is up here or anything like that, okay? I've heard it all."

Wow, you're tall!

Do you play basketball?

I bet you can always reach the top shelf with no problem!

"Jade, I still have an inch on you barefoot. Not that I care. Was it rough in school?"

"Sometimes." *So many times.* "It was better once I got into sports."

"Let me guess…basketball?"

She chuckled. "Yup. I resisted until I was a sophomore, only because everyone kept telling me I *should* be a basketball player." She gave him a look, remembering his comments about her stubbornness. "I was obstinate even then. But the coach encouraged me, and it was one of the few places where I fit in. And frankly, I was good at it. And it got me through a D1 college for free."

"Scholarship-worthy in Division One, huh? That's impressive."

She'd found a place to belong in college basketball. Her team had been tight knit. They were a group of tall, athletic, competitive women who'd each been the tallest girl in high school back home—not necessarily a fun time. High school girls could be catty and downright mean. She'd been teased about her height, or just shunned because kids didn't know how to react to having a classmate who towered almost a foot over their heads.

Then she got to college and ended up being one of the *shorter* women on the team, and it was a revelation. She didn't feel like she had to hunch her shoulders to take up less space. She could stand tall, and she could definitely hold her own on the basketball court. The team became a unit, and they'd gone all the way to be one of the final eight teams in the national playoffs in her junior year. Sadly, being part of *that* team had made her even more of an outsider at home.

Marla and Ashley were not athletes in any sense of the word. Too much risk of breaking a fingernail.

"You didn't want to go pro?"

She stretched her legs, patting her left knee. Under her leggings, it was crisscrossed with scars. "Ironically, I'm a little short for the pros, but I would have tried if I hadn't blown out my knee my senior year of college. For the second time in three years." The injury had taken her from campus stardom to anonymity in a matter of weeks. But she'd earned her business degree debt-free, then went on to culinary school.

Trent stared for a moment, his eyes warming her skin. "I hope our daughter inherits your talents." Her heart jumped in her chest. There was something about the interest and caring in Trent's expression that shook her to her core. She was going to have to be more careful around him, or she'd find herself falling for the guy she kept insisting she didn't need.

She stood, eager to move away from this highly personal conversation. "Do you want a sandwich or anything? Joe made some great ciabatta rolls this morning, and I have sliced turkey."

Jade heard the roaring in her ears right before her vision blurred. She'd stood up too fast, and her blood pressure was plummeting. She bit the inside of her lower lip *hard*, trying to keep her wits about her. The last thing she needed was to pass out in front of Trent. Or pass out at all.

"Holy sh—" Trent jumped up, sliding his arm around her waist. "You're white as a ghost. *Jade?*"

She fought with everything she had to stay awake, but her knees buckled. Trent held on, turning with her and helping her reach the sofa instead of hitting the floor. She blinked, and felt herself coming back from the edge of unconsciousness. Her heart was still pounding, but the roaring sound was fading and the room had stopped spinning. Trent sat next to her. She reached out to pat his arm, but missed, hitting his thigh instead.

"I'm okay," she whispered. "I'm okay."

"The hell you are," he growled. "Do I need to call an ambulance?"

Her clarity returned full-strength. "No! I'm fine, Trent. I stood up too quickly, that's all. Low blood pressure during pregnancy isn't uncommon, or so my doctor tells me." She glanced at the bottle of water she'd barely touched while they were talking. "I need to stay hydrated and I'm not supposed to change positions too quickly." She sat up and pushed herself back—she'd barely made the sofa cushion, even with Trent's help. "I'm better—no more dizziness. I promise."

He stared hard into her eyes as if to verify what

she'd said, then gave a slight nod. He reached for the bottle and opened it, pushing it into her hand.

"You're telling me your doctor *told* you that you were at risk, and that you should drink water and watch what you're doing, and you just decided you knew better?" He tapped the water bottle. "Drink that right now. All of it."

She drained half the bottle and paused for a breath. "This wasn't me being defiant. I just forget sometimes. And it's never been that bad before. Usually I just feel a little dizzy, then it passes."

"Drink," he ordered. "Is that what happened on Tuesday when I walked into the bakery, when you wobbled a bit?"

She started to answer, but he pointed to the bottle. She emptied it obediently. Defying him would only hurt herself, and possibly Bunny. She held up the empty bottle to prove she'd listened.

"I think shock had a lot to do with what happened Tuesday." To her surprise, Trent stood and took her ankles, swinging them gently up onto the sofa so she was reclining. Even more surprising, she had no desire to fight him. She settled into the cushions as a wave of exhaustion—or spent adrenaline—washed over her.

He frowned down at her. "Have you eaten lunch?" His eyes narrowed when she gave a guilty shrug. "Unbelievable. I'll make *you* that turkey sandwich. And I'll bring you another water. You stay put."

"Don't bring another sparkling water—Bunny doesn't like it when I get gassy, so I only have one a day. A glass of tap water would be great." He stared at her without moving. "What?"

"You sure you're okay? You scared the daylights out of me, Jade."

"Sorry." She flashed a quick smile. "You don't know how rare it is for anyone to hear that word twice in one day from me. I feel fine now. Although I could really use that sandwich."

He blew out a long breath, as if he'd been holding it since she almost fainted in his arms.

"I'm on it."

The sofa faced away from the kitchen so she couldn't see him, but she heard him opening and closing cupboards and drawers. She pushed back into the cushions and closed her eyes. It had been a long, stressful week, and she'd been careless with her self-care. That couldn't happen again.

Now here she was, allowing Trent to take care of her. Who would ever guess she'd allow *that* to happen? She listened to the father of her baby, humming to himself in the kitchen while he fixed her a late lunch. Almost like they were a family.

Trent's hands were shaking as he cut the ciabatta rolls. He tried to remember the last time he'd felt a spike of fear so powerful that it left him trembling afterward. Maybe a rock-climbing misstep or two in his earlier years, but nothing as innocuous as a woman nearly fainting. She *hadn't* fainted—Jade was fine, the baby was fine, he was fine. So why was the bread knife still going back and forth in his hand like he was directing an orchestra?

He set the knife down, braced his hands on the counter and closed his eyes. In a matter of days, he'd gone from being a carefree—if slightly unfulfilled—bachelor to being a father-to-be with a woman he barely knew. The same near-stranger who'd somehow managed to take ten years off his life by almost passing out in front of him. He pulled in a long breath through his nose and blew it out from his mouth, trying to settle his nerves.

Damn. If he couldn't handle a woman fainting, how was he going to handle raising a *child*?

Jade's face had paled so quickly he hadn't been sure it was real. But the moment her shoulders swayed, there was no doubt—she was in trouble. He'd managed to support her long enough to swing her onto the sofa, where she'd seemed to pull herself back to consciousness by sheer willpower. His daughter's mother was a force of nature.

He straightened and got back to work on the sandwiches. He found lettuce and tomatoes in the fridge, as well as the turkey, some slices of swiss cheese and mayo. He grimaced. He was a Miracle Whip guy himself. The sandwich plates were above the dishwasher. He set her sandwich, and a few of her beloved kettle chips, on a plate and filled a glass with cold water before delivering her lunch to her.

But she was sound asleep. Trent stood and watched her for a moment. Her long, black eyelashes were soft against her cheeks. Her lips were barely parted, and she was taking slow, deep breaths, her chest rising and falling. He set the sandwich and water on the side table and tugged at the soft throw blanket on the back of the sofa, covering her with it. He slid her shoes off, then frowned when he saw her ankles were swollen.

He could sneak out and leave her sleeping there, but it didn't feel right. What if she got up and passed out for *real* the next time? Instead, he brought his sandwich and a bottle of soda into the living area. He didn't sit in the chair—it was too far away from her. Instead, he lifted her feet and took a seat at that end of the sofa, putting her feet in his lap and tucking the blanket around them. At least now they were elevated a bit. He ate his sandwich and watched her sleep. Her baby bump—*his* baby—was right there within reach, but he knew it would be wrong to touch her. Even though he'd already seen, and kissed, every inch of her before. It was different now.

He watched the sun setting through the tall wall of windows. Gallant Lake turned shades of gold and pink as the sun moved lower. Across the street, there was a small park on the water with an ornate white gazebo. It took on the colors of the sunset, looking almost magical. There was a row of buildings on either side of the park, matching the ones on this side of Main Street. They were all well-kept older buildings, like something out of a 1930s movie, in clapboard or brick. The old-fashioned lampposts had dried cornstalks tied to them. Halloween was next week, and then Thanksgiving would follow a few weeks later. He glanced at Jade.

Christmas would be right after that, and then…his daughter would be born in the cold of January. Was there a hospital in town? Doubtful. Nearby? He'd have to find out. Jade did say she had a doctor, so it's not like this little town was completely isolated from civilization and safety. An older couple walked down the sidewalk on the far side of the street, then over to the gazebo. Both wore knit caps and jeans, with snug jackets to ward against the chill. The woman had a long braid of pewter-colored hair hanging down her back. They stopped at the gazebo steps and stared out at the lake before the man pulled her in for a long embrace, punctuated with an equally long kiss.

It was a scene straight out of some schmaltzy TV romance movie. But instead of rolling his eyes, he smiled. Gallant Lake felt like a moment out of time—charming, friendly, quirky, safe. The couple was still wrapped in each other's arms. He shook his head. And romantic. It felt like a good place to raise a family…he frowned. To raise a *child*. If Jade planned on raising their daughter here, he couldn't think of an objection. Other than it was a *long* way from Denver.

He'd made light of it earlier, but the fact was, traveling back and forth to see… *Bunny*, was going to be a pain. Not that it wouldn't be worth it, but the traveling itself would be expensive and time-consuming. He sipped the soda and watched the couple outside hurry down the sidewalk as darkness began to fall, presumably headed for warmth somewhere together.

Trent's mind spun as he analyzed his options. One thing he knew for sure was that he wasn't going to get on a plane this week and leave. He looked over at Jade, still sound asleep. He couldn't…not yet.

He pulled out his phone and texted Leonard Baxter, saying he needed even more time than he'd anticipated with that Albany client. Like…maybe a few weeks. Hopefully he could extend his room reservation that long.

It wasn't as if he intended to shirk the job, even if he didn't like dealing with mining and logging companies in general. He'd meet them and see what they needed. He'd probably just have to glad-hand some bureaucrat in the capital to resolve whatever their conflict was.

Jade's feet were still across his lap, and he began to rub one of them, gently stroking the arch with his fingers. She was working too hard. She wouldn't *care* what he thought, of course, but he couldn't help worrying anyway. There had to be some way he could make things easier for her without ruffling her prickly pride.

A little extra time in Gallant Lake would help him come up with a solution to his Jade problem.

Chapter Ten

Jade was having the nicest dream. Someone was giving her a foot rub. And It. Was. Heavenly. Strong hands moved up and down one foot at a time, gripping and releasing. Running a knuckle down her arch firmly enough to send a shiver all the way up her body. Then massaging her toes gently. And her ankles.

Good God, this feels good...

A car horn blew down on the street, making her flinch. *No!* She didn't want to wake up. This was too perfect. But it was all in vain. She was awake. Her eyes swept open. She'd fallen asleep on the sofa again. It was dark outside, but luckily she'd left the kitchen light on. She frowned. She didn't remember turning on that light.

And someone was still rubbing her feet.

She pulled away with a gasp, kicking out at whoever was in her apartment, touching her *feet*.

"Ow! Damn it, Jade. *Ow!*" She heard familiar male laughter. "You kick like a mule!"

"Trent?" She was fully awake now. He must have still been there when she fell asleep. "Oh my God, I fell asleep while you were making sandwiches, didn't I?" She looked at the dark windows again. "What time is it?"

"It's after seven. You fell asleep around four." He reached for her foot, giving her a sideways glance. "You done kicking now?"

"Hey, I was scared, okay? I thought I was dreaming, and then realized there was someone in my house, touching my feet for real. Why are you here?" She allowed him to take her foot back, because the man was a *master* foot-rubber and she wasn't stupid. He started massaging again, doing that magical thing on her arch that made her groan out loud. His hand stopped at the sound, then started moving again.

"It felt like a dick move to leave. I wanted to make sure you were okay." He took her other foot and massaged it, and she sighed. The corner of his mouth lifted. "Want me to go?"

"I want you to rub my feet like that for *hours*." No sense denying it, since she'd let out those groans of pleasure. "Look, it was...nice...of you to stay. But I'm okay. That fainting thing was a total fluke."

"You'll have to prove the *fluke* part to me. Drink that water, eat something and then we'll see how you do standing."

"Don't you have packing to do?" She'd originally thought she couldn't *wait* for him to leave. Now the idea left a tiny shadow on her heart.

"Uh…not yet." He hesitated. "We have a client in Albany who needs legal advice, so I'm hanging around."

She studied him. "Because of the client or because of me?" She wasn't sure what she wanted his answer to be.

He looked over at her, his eyes solemn. "Both, I guess. I need to make sure we have a plan in place, Jade." He talked over her objection. "Yes, I know you *can* do it yourself. You are strong and independent and thoroughly capable. You have a good support circle here in Gallant Lake. But we agreed that I'd be a jerk if I didn't want to be involved in my daughter's life, so I'm afraid you'll have to get used to my opinions…take 'em or leave 'em."

She gently—and regretfully—pulled her feet from his lap and moved to sit up. He reached out to steady her, but she glared at his hand and he pulled it back with a quick grin.

"Let me guess," he said. "You're fine."

She took a long drink of water. "I really *am*, you know." She looked around the room, quietly testing her dizziness level. No spinning or blurriness. No roar in her ears. She felt steady and normal. "But I am also hungry." She stood, and he jumped to his feet, ready to catch her. "For God's sake, back off." She turned in a circle to prove her point. "I told you it was a fluke." She headed for the kitchen, with Trent right behind her.

"I covered your sandwich and put it in the fridge. Have a seat and I'll get it for you. Do you want anything else with it? Do you have soup or anything?"

She was set to tell him to leave her alone until he mentioned soup. That sounded really good, and she had tomato soup in the cupboard.

"There's soup next to the stove. Something warm sounds great."

He nodded. "How about I grill that sandwich real quick? Make it a turkey melt?"

"First you rub my feet and now you're offering to make me comfort food? Careful, Trent—I might just get used to having you around." She sat at the island and watched him at work, unaccustomed to being waited on. He was no restaurant chef, but he knew his way around a kitchen. In about ten minutes, she had a pressed turkey and cheese melt and hot soup. There were kettle chips, too, but she gave him a rueful smile. "That particular craving has passed, but thanks anyway. I'm sure I'll want them again at some point."

Trent poured himself a mugful of soup. They talked about the environmental conference while she ate. He explained that it was a gathering of climate experts and advocates from many fields, from farming to industry, journalism to law. Jade told him she'd heard that Blake Randall had been instrumental in putting it together, and that he'd recently installed solar panels on the roof of both the resort and the golf club.

Trent asked about the Randalls' castle home, the one named Halcyon. Jade shared what she knew—Blake's original plan had been to raze both the castle *and* the resort to build a casino. The locals had fought him and won the historic designation for Halcyon. Then he'd hired Amanda to renovate it into a home for him and his orphaned nephew, Zach. Blake and Amanda fell in love, adopted Zach, had daughter Maddie, and all thoughts of a casino were forgotten. Instead, they updated the existing resort, adding a golf course and, more recently, vacation condominiums on an adjacent property. The resort had brought new life—and new jobs—to the area, and Gallant Lake was beginning to boom.

"That's why you thought a bakery would succeed here?" he asked.

"The old bakery closed before the resort turned things around. Everyone said the town needed one. I'd come to the realization that I needed to put some distance between my family and I. I had a small inheritance, and it went farther here than in St. Louis, which was a big plus." She took a last bite of her sandwich. "The only thing not in my business plan was Bunny." She patted her belly. "But once I get past the next few months, I think it's going to work out." She nodded toward a white bakery box on the counter. "There are some day-old pastries in there."

Trent retrieved the box and sat next to her again, opening it with a laugh. "Whoa—this is like the mother lode of sweetness." He took a kataifi and examined it. "This looks like a shredded breakfast cereal." He took a bite, closing his eyes and moaning. "It tastes like…shredded baklava?"

She nodded. "Kataifi has honey and nuts just like baklava."

"You got all these recipes from your mom's side of the family?"

"Yes, I remember eating my mom's baking as a kid, and then my grandmother taught me how to make everything when I'd visit her in Chicago. It's where I got my love of pastry making." A ripple went across her abdomen, and the piece of baklava she'd taken fell to the plate as she gasped. Trent grabbed her arm in alarm.

"What is it? Are you dizzy again?" He stood and moved behind her, close enough to support her if needed. She leaned against him, even though she didn't really need to.

"I'm not having a fainting spell." She took his right hand and moved it toward her stomach. He started to resist, then allowed her to flatten his hand on the front of her sweater. "I don't know if you'll be able to feel it or not, but Bunny is moving. It's the most I've felt her so far...oh!" Another ripple, and the sensation of bubbles inside her. A move from left to right as the baby seemed to relocate herself inside of Jade. And then again, in the other direction. Jade laughed. "I think she's going to be a swimmer!"

Trent was very still. Bunny's next move brought her forward and made it feel as if she was right under Jade's skin for just a flutter of movement. Trent's eyes went round, and color drained from his cheeks.

"That's *her*?" His voice was hushed, as if afraid to scare the baby. "That little vibration?"

Jade chuckled. "It better be. If not, I'm having the worst gas attack *ever*."

The baby made one last move to the left, moving farther inside with a single swirling motion. Jade's heart filled with emotion. She was carrying *life*.

She turned to look into Trent's eyes. She saw the same emotions she was feeling reflected there—awe, gratitude, love. Her daughter would be loved. Protected. She pressed back against his chest, and his arms circled around her, his fingers brushing her baby bump.

"She's done for now," Jade whispered. "That was quite a little somersault she did."

"Holy..." Trent was whispering, too. His face was right next to hers, so close their noses were almost brushing. "Jade…that was incredible. She's moving. She's—"

"Strong," she finished. "She's strong and healthy."

His gaze met hers. So close that she could see the flecks of copper in his honey-colored eyes. Would Bunny have his eyes? She hoped so.

"Trent…" She breathed his name, suddenly lost in those gold-gilded eyes. His arms tightened around her. He touched her chin with his fingertips, tilting her face toward him.

"It's not surprising that our daughter is already strong and feisty and awe-inspiring, just like her mom."

Despite his words, Jade had a feeling he wasn't really talking—or thinking—about their daughter anymore. He searched her face, so close his lips barely brushed hers. She couldn't help smiling.

"Awe-inspiring, huh?" She moved her head so that their lips touched again, ever so slightly. She remembered him being a *very* good kisser. And she could really use a good kiss right now. Another pregnancy craving? Maybe. If so, she should probably satisfy it so it didn't spin out of control. His mouth smiled against hers.

"I remember a night when you were definitely awe-inspiring, Jade. Beautiful. Passionate." He turned his head and kissed her upper lip. "Smart. Funny.

And sexy as hell. And you know what?" He kissed her lower lip now.

"What?" She practically gasped the question, unexpected desire rising like gasoline-fueled flames inside of her.

"You're still all of those things. Please tell me it's okay to kiss you, because I really, *really* want to kiss you right now."

She didn't answer—she just reached up to cup the back of his head with her hand and pulled him in. Their mouths melded together like long-lost lovers. Firm, tender, intense…filled with longing. They both moaned at the same time as their mouths opened and the kiss deepened, their tongues pushing together. She surrendered, allowing him to take full ownership.

She'd had plenty of kisses in her life, but no one made her feel the way Trent made her feel. Like she was on fire. Like she'd never get enough of him. She'd been telling herself for months that her dreamy memories of kissing Trent were colored by the intensity of that emotional wedding night back in April. But here she was, tired and pregnant, sitting on a kitchen stool, and his kiss was every bit as good as she'd remembered. There was a low growl in his throat as he lifted one hand to the back of her head and held her in place. He didn't want this to end any more than she did.

Minutes melted together as they continued exploring, only parting long enough to catch a breath before returning to the kiss. It was Trent who finally pulled away, dropping his head to breathe heavily against her neck, then nuzzling her there, too. She whispered his name and he lifted his head, looking as confused and ravaged as she felt.

"So," she said, smiling, "we still have chemistry."

He brushed a kiss on her forehead. "Girl, we've got a whole science laboratory of chemistry. Not a high school lab, either. I'm talking mega-corporate science lab that takes up a whole building with every bell and whistle imaginable."

"No argument here." She snickered. "No wonder we managed to conceive in one night."

She felt his hesitation more than saw it. Did he *still* not believe this baby was his? Jade pulled back, putting her hand on his chest. The chemistry had evaporated.

"Trent, this is *your* baby. It is absolutely impossible for it to be anyone else's. What would be the point of me lying to you?"

Trent closed his eyes, his jaw going hard and tight. "I believe you. I *do*. That was just a kneejerk reaction. Sorry. It's just…" He rubbed the back of his neck, staring at the counter. "I've been burned before, okay? I'm talking *flamethrower* burned. The type of damage that leaves a lot of scars."

She saw the pain in his face, and her heart softened. "Your divorce? Do you want to talk about it?"

"Not even a little."

Trent stepped back, needing more space. Being in Jade's presence was like riding the world's wildest roller coaster—warm and familiar one minute, then on-fire hot, or off-the-rails terrifying. He cleared his throat loudly, trying to regroup. His answer had been abrupt, but he'd come very close to oversharing and that couldn't happen.

"I...uh...should probably go."

"Yeah, sure." Her expression cooled. The moment was broken. "How long did you say you were staying in Gallant Lake?"

"As long as I need to. We have unfinished business, Jade. Or at least, unfinished conversations."

"About whoever burned you?"

"That's a hard no." He started to scowl, then saw the hurt in her expression. He sighed instead, staring at the floor. "Someday, maybe. But...not right now. I don't want it creeping into my current life."

He didn't want memories of Cindy anywhere near Jade.

She tipped her head so she could look up into his eyes. "I just have to point out that if you're bringing it up, it's *already* creeping into your current life."

He snorted. "Maybe I should fire my therapist and

hire you." He thought about what he'd just said and held up his hands. "On second thought, no thanks."

She grinned. "Coward! So what are these unfinished conversations you think we need to have?"

"We still have a lot to learn about each other, Jade. I think that's important if we're going to do this together." He nodded toward her rounded stomach, where he'd just felt a child...*his* child...do somersaults.

"We don't have to do anything *together*." Her smile slowly faded. "I meant what I said. I can raise her alone."

"And I meant what *I* said," he replied. "I'm not the kind of man who'd ever let that happen."

"But seriously...how long *are* you staying?" She didn't seem keen on the idea.

He shrugged. "Enough time to wrap my head around what's happening. Enough time for us to spend time together..." He thought of the kiss they'd just shared and shook his head. "Not *that* kind of time."

She started laughing. "I didn't say a damn thing, so who are you warning? I'm thinking I was right in calling you a coward, Trent Michaels."

They stared at each other, the air suddenly charged with sexual tension again. Apparently it didn't matter how close they were to each other. Just the suggestion of intimacy was enough to start the fireworks.

Retreat! Retreat!

"I think it's time for me to head back to the resort. Do you want to… I don't know…do something tomorrow? Dinner?" He ran his fingers through his hair, and a honey-colored shock fell across his forehead. "This is hella awkward, isn't it?"

When they got to the back door, she folded her arms on her chest. "We're going to be parents together, and we kiss really well, but that doesn't make us a couple or anything. We're not dating. We don't need to be joined at the hip. I don't need a keeper."

His hand rested on the doorknob. "Considering you nearly passed out in my arms earlier, I'm not sure that's true. But if you're saying you need a little space, I can do that. Why don't you call me when you're ready to talk about making plans."

She thought for a moment. "That's fair. I'm not putting you off, but my weekdays are really busy, and I think… I think we need to go slow."

"I'll let you manage the timeline, Jade."

He opened the door, kicking himself for handing all the control to her. But he saw the way her posture had eased, her arms dropping to her sides. She needed this. And she was right—they weren't dating. And he *did* have work to do in Albany. He could always drop by the bakery without being a stalker-boy. Just to say hi. She wanted space, but she never said she didn't ever want to see him again.

Thank God…because that would have been really hard to agree to.

Chapter Eleven

Jade parked her car in front of Halcyon, the palatial home of Blake and Amanda Randall. It was time for the holiday planning meeting of the business-women of Gallant Lake, and Amanda was hosting the annual luncheon. It was Wednesday—they held it midweek to make it easier to leave their businesses—weekends were busy in a resort town.

Mayor Mary Andrews and her wife Julia were getting out of their car as Jade pulled in. The mayor had a law office in town, and Julia had an accounting business with offices in Gallant Lake and Kingston. They'd both welcomed Jade and the bakery just as warmly as everyone else in town.

They waved and hurried over to help Jade with the trays of pastries she'd brought for dessert.

"Do you think anyone would notice if we tucked both these trays in our car and just went home?" Julia asked, taking a deep sniff of the baklava. Her short dreads, many tipped with wooden beads, swayed as she dipped her head. "This smells too good to be real."

"We need to share with the other ladies, babe." The mayor laughed. "But boy, am I glad Jade Malone belongs to our business group now." She winked at Jade.

They walked into the castle together. The other women were already gathered in the sunlit atrium, where there was a happy buzz of laughter and conversation. She'd been introduced to this group early on—they jokingly referred to themselves as Women Who Got Things Done. In the beginning, it was just the Lowery cousins, but as Gallant Lake grew, so did the number of women creating businesses in town.

Nora told her they'd started putting together a calendar a few years ago for retail events between Thanksgiving week and Christmas, with a different theme every year. They'd chip in for decorations on Main Street, coordinate sales and giveaways, and do their best to make little Gallant Lake into a holiday must-see. Most of the businesses participated in a decorating competition. This year's theme was "Toyland," with children's Christmas fantasies featured all around. Mel glanced toward Jade during the meeting.

"Sounds perfect for our newest member."

The other women laughed, raising their glasses in a toast. Jade raised her orange juice in return.

"If you could all use *real* toys as decorations, I'll be accepting donations after Christmas. It'll save me a shopping trip."

More laughter, then they finished the business portion of the meeting and Amanda served a lunch buffet. As Jade was going through the line, Mack leaned close. "Trent was in the store yesterday picking up a bottle of scotch. How long is he staying around?"

That was a very good question. He'd given her complete control over when they'd see each other again. And she hadn't called. She wasn't sure why—was she trying to prove to him or to *herself* that she didn't need him in her life?

It hadn't been total silence on his part—he'd texted at least once a day to make sure she was drinking water and eating. She'd always texted back that she was fine, knowing it would make him roll his eyes in that cute way he had.

"Jade?" Mack asked. "Has he said how long he's staying?"

"You'll have to ask *him*." She hadn't meant to sound that sharp. "Sorry. I just meant I haven't talked to him." She scooped some roasted brussels sprouts onto her plate. "Not much, anyway."

He'd even stopped by the bakery over the weekend to buy a box of pastries. He'd been laid-back and friendly, asking how she was and examining her to make sure she was standing without assistance. But he hadn't pushed her. He'd stayed true to his word, which…meant something.

Her avoiding him this long was silly. He was clearly not going to pack up and leave, forgetting about her or his daughter. Whether she wanted to have him around or not, he was Bunny's father. Holding him at bay would accomplish nothing.

Mack followed Jade back to the table. She was in a chatty mood. "Trent told Dan he's looking at rental places around town. He said he might take one of Blake's vacation townhouses for a few months."

"For a few *months*?" Jade dropped her cool routine. She almost dropped her plate. "What about his job? How can he stay here for *months*?"

Mack gave her a pointed look. "I don't know. I guess you'll have to ask *him*."

Jade's shoulders fell. "It's not like we had a fight or anything. He offered to give me…*space*…or control or…*something* and I took it…" The next move was hers.

Mack chewed her sandwich thoughtfully for a moment. "So he thinks you *want* space, but you don't *really* want space, so why can't you just *tell* him you don't want space anymore so you two can talk?"

Jade started to laugh in spite of herself. "All I have to do is figure out if I want this guy in my *life* or not."

Mack made a show of leaning over to look at Bunny. "I think that ship has sailed. That man is in your life, one way or the other."

There was no arguing with that fact. And a partner would be helpful, considering she had no idea how to be a parent. But Jade had always been a lone wolf. Her last boss had laughingly put a little sign near her pastry station that read *Does not play well with others*.

She changed the subject, turning to their tablemates, including the mayor and her wife. They were talking about doing some kind of winter festival or something for Valentine's Day. The resort always had a Sweethearts Weekend in February, so maybe the businesses in town could tie into that.

The luncheon was breaking up when Mack began coughing, her eyes wide. She was staring at the entrance to the atrium. "Um…looks like you should decide that thing about space pretty quick. 'Cause he's here."

Jade turned and her pulse jumped. There was a group of men at the door who were just beginning to catch the attention of the rest of the women's group. Trent was next to Blake, saying something to a man Jade didn't recognize. Dan was there, along with the golf pro, Quinn Walker, and Nora's husband, Asher. Nick West was laughing, his arm around the shoulder of Matt Danzer, who owned the local ski lodge.

A few cheers and catcalls were rising from the

women. The guys did look pretty damn sexy. They knew it, too—they were basically flaunting it in their Henleys, flannel shirts, jeans and hiking boots.

"Wow," Mack sighed. "Gallant Lake sure has some hot men."

Mack's husband Dan looked good, but Jade only had eyes for Trent. His flannel sleeves were rolled up, exposing taut forearms. His eyes were locked on her. Golden and laser-focused. A gaze that held her frozen in place.

"Where have they been?" she asked Mack softly. The men's faces were ruddy from the sun, their hair windblown.

"Dan said they were going to help Matt clear the trails to the snow-making machines on the slopes and get ready for ski season. And I'm pretty sure they planned on taking a few trips down the zipline while they were there, since it's such a bracing November day and they're such manly men." Mack's eyelashes fluttered and she pretended to fan herself. "We really need to do a calendar of hot Gallant Lake guys some year."

"Ladies." Blake held up his hand, laughing as the catcalls increased. "Sorry to interrupt this important gathering. We're headed to the kitchen to scope out the leftovers, and thought we'd check to see if you've volunteered us for any tasks downtown this year."

"Oh, bummer!" Julie Brown, the resort manager shouted through cupped hands held to her mouth like a megaphone. "We thought you were the entertainment!" The room burst into laughter. Julie ran over to hug her fiancé, Quinn. "And yes, we signed you guys up to hang the garlands on the gazebo, and the bunting on the lampposts, and the banner across Main Street…"

The mayor shook her head. "The town maintenance crews will take care of the banner and the lampposts, but if the men's group could decorate the gazebo and the park, that would be great." She winked at the lunching ladies. "And I'm sure those of you whose wives own businesses downtown will be recruited to help decorate the store windows for our annual competition."

Some of the men groaned, and Blake started to lead them toward the kitchen. But Trent lingered, waiting. Jade walked over to him, taking his arm and pulling him along with her as she headed into the family room overlooking the lake.

"Is there a problem?" Trent asked as they stepped into the room and she closed the massive doors behind them.

"Yeah, there's a problem. The problem is *you*. Still in Gallant Lake. Looking at *rental* properties. What are you doing, Trent?"

"Umm…living my life? Why are you so ticked off?"

"Why didn't you tell me you were freakin' *moving* here?"

They faced each other in the middle of the room.

"For one thing, I don't know if I'm moving here or not. I'm just...exploring options. And I didn't *tell* you because you're the one controlling when we talk to each other right now. If you'd called, I would have told you." He jammed his fingers through his hair. "What'd you think I was going to do in the meantime—sit on the edge of my bed waiting for the phone to ring?"

Perfectly reasonable. And so annoying.

"So you're just—" she gestured back toward the rest of the house "—hanging out with the guys, making friends like you're a local now?"

He folded his arms on his chest. She really wished he wouldn't do that. It was very distracting.

"You're mad because I'm making friends?"

She threw her hands in the air. "I'm mad because...because..." She took a deep breath, trying to calm herself. "I guess I'm more surprised than mad. How can you possibly be thinking of relocating to Gallant Lake? What about your law firm?"

He stared at her, then dropped his arms with a heavy sigh. He nodded to the pair of chairs near the French doors facing the water. "Why don't you sit down. We have a lot to catch up on."

"Clearly," she drawled. "But this is someone else's house. They all talk about us enough as it is. Let's go back out and act normal, and we can..." She stumbled over the invite, remembering that steaming kiss in her kitchen ten days ago. She licked her lower lip, then saw the way his eyes went dark. This would be a bad idea. But she finished the sentence anyway. "We can go back to my place later and talk." She held up a finger. "Just talk."

"Yes, ma'am." He stepped back with a bemused grin and let her lead the way back to their friends.

Their friends. She wasn't sure how she felt about sharing friends with Trent. Maybe that was why she'd been so mad earlier. It wasn't that he was making friends, but that he was making friends with *her* friends. The larger group had broken up and gone home, but they found three couples—Blake and Amanda, Julie and Quinn, Nora and Asher—working in the kitchen to clean up and put things away. As big as this house was, Amanda ran it with very little help.

"Oh, there you are!" Amanda looked up when they walked in. "Trent, I put a sandwich plate together for you, and there's a beer there, too. Jade, another orange juice?"

Trent grabbed at the sandwich like a starving man and gobbled it down. The guys talked about the work they'd done at the lodge all morning, and then, just as Mack had guessed—how much fun they'd had using some of the long ziplines that kept the lodge going during the summer months.

The women finished putting the serving dishes

away in the pantry cupboard. Julie looked over to where the guys were sitting.

"Trent seems like a really great guy, Jade."

She followed Julie's gaze and smiled in spite of herself. He was perched on the edge of the kitchen table, deep into telling a story. From his hand gestures, he was describing some rock climbing adventure. It reminded her of that first night, when they'd sat on the picnic table and talked. He'd been more than just sexy that night—he'd been kind and charming. Caring.

At that moment in his story, something funny must have happened, because his hands went wide and his facial expression looked shocked. All the guys burst out laughing, including Trent.

"Yes, I think he *is* a pretty good guy." Jade nodded. Trent looked up and their eyes met for just a moment, but it was enough for her to feel all those things from that April night all over again—cared for. Respected. And desired. Maybe *space* hadn't been what they'd needed at all. She'd called him a coward the last time he was in her apartment, but she was beginning to think *she* was the one who was driven by fear.

That fear made sense when she didn't know the guy. When he was nothing more than a steamy moonlit memory. She'd had no idea what kind of man he really was. But so far, he'd been exactly the same guy he'd been for those precious hours back in April.

Nora stepped up next to her, her voice low. "You coulda' done worse for a one-night stand. My Asher doesn't warm up to new friends easily, but he's already invited Trent to the weekly poker games at the shop."

If Jade was going to raise her daughter here, it was a *good* thing that Trent got along with her friends. She might have her doubts about him *moving* here, but she couldn't point to any specific reason why he shouldn't do it if he wanted to.

But they still needed to talk. She caught his eye again and gave a nod toward the door.

Trent convinced her to let him drive her car down to town. It was a nice enough day that he could walk back up to the resort later.

He noticed she was low on fuel, so he turned toward the gas station up on the main highway. She grumbled a little, but agreed it was a good idea to actually have gasoline in the tank.

"I found a nice little cafe over in Hudson," he said as he drove, "with great views of the Hudson River. Maybe we could have a late lunch there sometime." She stared over at him, and he laughed. "What?"

"How did you happen to scout out a nice cafe three towns away?"

"I…uh…had a job interview there last week."

"Ex*cuse* me?"

He chuckled. "I told you we had a lot to catch up

on. And it was more of a meet-and-greet sort of thing. No job yet."

"You're actually job-hunting here?"

"Well, a man's gotta eat. I…um…quit my old firm in Denver." Jade's eyes narrowed. "Before you freak out, I've been thinking about doing this for a long time. Not moving to the Catskills, but moving out of corporate law and into environmental law."

"That's why you came to the conference? To job hunt?"

"To at least explore options, yeah." They drove past a large farm with a maple syrup stand near the road, and he pointed toward it. "A friend of Dan's owns that place. He says their syrup is the best. You should check it out."

"Paul and Scott? Great idea. That's where I source my maple syrup, genius. I can't believe *you* know about it already." She gave him a wide smile. "Your superpower is making social connections fast. I'm impressed."

His ability to quickly find common ground with people had smoothed a lot of negotiations over the years—attract more bees with honey and all that. He knew it was a strength of his, but hearing Jade call it a *superpower* almost made him want to preen. Her opinion of him mattered more than it probably should.

They talked about some of the other discoveries he'd made in the short time he'd been in the area—

the llama farm, the ski lodge, the locally legendary Kissing Rock up on Gallant Mountain. The Catskills were different from the Rockies, but no less beautiful. And just as much in need of protection. Maybe even more so, considering the population centers encroaching from New York City to the south, Albany to the north and Connecticut to the east.

He parked her car behind her apartment and tried to scramble fast enough to open her door, but she was too quick for him. Miss Independent was already out and headed up the stairs. "So you think you can find a rewarding job in Gallant Lake? Or even in Hudson?"

Vince Grassman was setting him up with a bunch of interviews, mostly with conservation groups in the northeast. Vince had joined the guys today at the ski lodge, and had given Trent a few new leads. It was just a matter of finding the right fit for the right money.

"I'll find something. People aren't tied to offices in specific locations anymore." He followed her into the apartment. "Sure, the courtrooms and jurisdictions are geographic places, but the prep work can be done almost anywhere." He did manage to help her with her coat, saving some of his chivalrous dignity. "And Albany's only an hour away."

"You had a client up there, right? How did that go?"

He grimaced. "Listening to their so-called plan

to cheat the system and get around logging regulations was the final straw for me. I didn't *like* the job I had, but I'd never had the motivation to make the move before now." He gave her a pointed look. "Again, you having our baby is not the only reason I quit, but having someone I wanted to be near... it was enough to finish opening that door for me."

And he wasn't just talking about the baby. He liked being around Jade. He sat at the kitchen island while she pulled a plate of pastries from the fridge. She held up a beer, but he opted for soda instead. "Once the door was open, I couldn't go through it fast enough. So technically, your baby daddy is unemployed."

She sat next to him with a soft laugh. "I sure know how to pick 'em."

"Don't worry about it."

"I'm not worried, Trent." She took a sip of her water. "I keep telling you I can raise Bunny on my own."

"And I keep telling you that's not going to happen. If this is my child, I'm going to step up financially as well as personally."

Her shoulders snapped back as if he'd struck her. "*If?* You quit your job to move here and you still don't believe me?"

Damn it. "I swear I didn't mean it like that. I believe you. Bunny is mine." And he truly *did* believe that, and not just because Jade had offered a DNA test. He just…knew. But his mouth apparently hadn't gotten the message. "Old habits die hard, I guess. I told you I've been burned before."

"Right. The divorce. What happened?"

They were *definitely* not going there. He shook his head. "Crashed and burned."

"And you really won't talk about it?"

"Not to you." He saw the hurt in her eyes and rushed to explain. "I just don't see an upside to rehashing it all over again." He pictured the barren house, empty of nearly every stick of furniture and all signs of the family that once called it home. "That's what therapy was for."

She stared at him, and he felt her trying to read his mind. "Well, whatever's causing your trust issues, it's sitting here between us, and I don't even know what it *is*, much less how to deal with it." She held his forearm, her fingers setting off warm little sparks on his skin. "So this…*something*…makes you think I somehow maneuvered to lure you back to Gallant Lake with a symposium I didn't know about and had no idea you'd be interested in, and then made it rain so you'd come into my bakery, all so I could blindside you with a paternity claim. You know that makes no sense, right?"

"I know. I'm just saying…we're still virtually strangers." He flashed a quick grin. "Strangers who have the hots for each other, but…neither of us has any idea what the other is really capable of." He blew out a long breath. "And let's be fair—you didn't plan on telling me I was the father. If I hadn't shown up, I'd never have known."

Jade thought for a moment, then sat up straight, her eyes brightening. "Wait—I can at least prove *that* isn't true. I mean, I'll admit I was waffling, but I was trying to figure out how to tell a total stranger we were going to have a baby together. Come with me."

She slid off the barstool and took his hand, leading him up the long flight of metal stairs that led to the upstairs loft. The upstairs loft that was her very feminine and inviting bedroom. He stopped at the top of the stairs.

"Get your mind out of the gutter and come over here." She tugged his hand, dragging him to the ornate writing table where her laptop sat. She opened her emails. There was one there addressed to him. "Check the date, Trent. It's two months ago."

"I never got an email from you." He'd have opened it for sure. But then, he wouldn't recognize her name, so maybe he'd missed it?

"I never *sent* it," Jade explained. "It's in my drafts folder. Once I tracked down your real name, it wasn't hard to get your work email. I wrote and rewrote this a dozen times. I had my finger on Send more times than that. I just wasn't sure if I should tell you about Bunny or not." She slid the laptop toward him. "I was afraid of all the possible complications if I told you." She laughed softly. "And then you showed up and complicated things anyway. Please…read it."

Trent was used to multitasking, but his brain was having a hard time keeping up right now. This woman had gone from a fantasy night to a very real, and *pregnant*, reality. Despite his doubts and her fierce independence, their attraction was still red-hot. Ten days ago they'd shared the Kiss to End All Kisses right before he'd stupidly offered to give her space. Now they were finally talking, and he'd let his doubts slip out again, ruining everything.

Or had it? Because right now, he was standing in her bedroom. Her bed was just a few feet behind where they were standing. This space was a contrast to the industrial loft vibe of the apartment, with a white iron bed and yards and yards of netting tumbling from the ceiling to create a soft, sensual atmosphere. Or maybe it was just Jade who did that.

But the multitasking wasn't done yet, because she was shoving a laptop into his hands, demanding he read a draft email she'd written over two months ago. It was important to her, so he did his best to forget the bed and focus on the screen.

In the email, she was reintroducing herself to him—as if he'd ever forget. In usual Jade fashion, she laid it all out without pretense in the email. She was pregnant. It was definitely his. She was keeping the child. She didn't want or need him to take on any parental role. She just thought he should be aware.

Trent tried to imagine what his reaction would be if he'd received that email out of the blue. Probably the same reaction he had here in Gallant Lake. Shock. And a large dose of skepticism. He knew where that came from.

Cindy's lies shouldn't have anything to do with trusting Jade. But the truth was, his experiences with Cindy colored everything. None of that was Jade's fault, though.

"Trent?" Jade touched his arm. "I admit I hesitated to tell you, but for totally selfish reasons. I don't do teamwork or partnering or co-anything very well. To be honest, I didn't want to share Bunny with anyone. In my mind, she was *mine*. But I knew as soon as you saw I was pregnant that I had to tell you."

He looked into her eyes, dark and shimmering with emotion, and he knew. He didn't need any DNA test. Her baby was his baby. His past wasn't going to ruin this for him. But he knew it would try.

He set the laptop on the desk and pulled Jade into his arms. "I'm glad you showed this to me. I'm also sorry I made you feel you had to. My screwed up past and all the angst it causes me doesn't diminish my feelings for you or our daughter."

Her mouth lifted into a teasing grin. "You have feelings for me?"

"I do." His embrace tightened. "I also have feelings about that bed sitting right behind you. It's bringing back some really great memories."

Jade glanced over her shoulder to the bed, then back to him.

"Wanna see if we still got it?"

Everything in the room went still and silent. Trent was pretty sure even his heart had stopped. He knew his breathing had. He looked down at her softly rounded stomach.

"Is that a good idea?"

"If you're asking if it's safe, the answer is yes. I've been assured she's very protected in there." Jade slid her arms around his neck. "If you're just asking my opinion, then also yes. I think it's a *very* good idea." Her lips touched his and that was all it took to erase any remaining questions.

His fingers twisted in her hair while he kissed her deep and hard. Her soft moan added to his urgency. He wanted more. He wanted *her*. Jade's hands were in his hair now, digging in. Holding on. Their desperation was equal.

It was one of the things he liked most about the two of them together, whether in conversation or in bed—they were right there, level with each other. No one was "in charge." They were on the same page, which made things that much more intimate. There was no need for words when they were both in sync like this.

Clothes came off. The bed was found. Blankets pulled down. Jade on her back, hair splayed out around her head like a dark halo. Her breasts...

"Whoa," he said, his hands sliding over them to tease her rigid peaks. "I didn't think these could get any better, but…pregnancy suits you."

She arched her back at his touch while still rolling her eyes at his comment. "Give me a few more months and you may think differently. But yes, the girls are definitely bigger these days."

He was straddling her now, on his knees and looking down at her long body with all of its lush new curves. He'd never seen anything in his life as beautiful as she was right now.

Her gaze met his and she gave him her slanted grin. "You gonna look all night or are you going to *do* something, big guy?"

God, he loved the way she challenged him all the time, even now. Jade sharpened him, perfected him. The way a whetstone sharpened a knife's edge.

His erection was hard and quivering. But there was something missing. He looked up at the ceiling and swore.

"I don't suppose a pregnant lady has any condoms lying around?"

Her laugh was husky and deep. "I don't suppose a pregnant lady needs to worry about getting pregnant, do you?" Her laughter faded. "Like I said, one time all year, and it was with you. Have you been a wild man since then? Or before?"

He shook his head slowly, realizing what she was saying. He lowered himself over her. "As you know,

I don't do unprotected sex. And there hasn't been anyone since…us." It had been a long dry spell for him, between work and knowing no woman would live up to the memories Jade gave him in April. "Are you sure?"

She lifted her head and kissed the base of his neck, then nipped it with her teeth, sending shock waves straight to the part of him waiting to enter her. He caught her mouth with his as he slid into her. They both let out matching moans as he filled her warmth and held in place, wanting to savor the feeling as long as possible.

But Jade had other ideas. She lifted up against him and their bodies began to move together. No thought required. Just automatically in tune with each other and knowing what the other needed. How was it possible that it was better than before? Would every time they made love just get better and better? Could his heart survive that? Because right now it felt like he was going to explode.

He drove into her, and she met him move for move, encouraging him with wordless sounds as the pace increased. Finally he couldn't take any more— he was afraid he might actually die from ecstasy. He buried his face in her shoulder and cried out as his world exploded in a kaleidoscope of fractured colors. Again. And again. She'd gone with him, her fingers digging deep into his back as she cried his name… or something that sounded like his name. But he was too focused on bringing his heart rate back down from the stratosphere.

"Holy mother of…" He gasped the words as if he'd just finished a marathon. "I can't even… Holy *hell*, Jade, that was incredible."

Her hand patted the back of his head like he was a dog. Pat, pat, pat.

"Yeah," she muttered. "Pretty damn good."

Pretty damn good? More like headline-making, fireworks-creating, lights-out sex. But he knew how she felt. Articulating with actual words via mouths and sound was difficult after sex like that. He slid off of her, pulling her close and tugging the blankets over them.

Pretty damn good would have to do. Until the next time. Which would happen just as soon as his body recovered.

Chapter Twelve

Jade felt the moment Trent fell asleep behind her, his breathing going soft and steady against her skin from between his parted lips. She was surprised she wasn't doing the same thing, but instead she felt energized. Her entire body was buzzing right beneath her skin. It was a happy energy. She stretched with a smile. A proud and deeply satisfied energy.

For all the times she'd wondered if that April night was just a fluke...well, it definitely was not. Turned out she and Trent had something *real* going on between them. Something more than chemistry. Chemistry was just a reaction *between* two elements. What they had was a *connection*. A no-communication-required connection that made things effortless. That made *them* effortless. That *changed* them.

She was a different person when she was naked in Trent Michaels's arms. Vulnerable, but not in a way that made her feel weak. Just…open. And equal. She turned in his arms, admired the sharp lines of his sleeping face, then kissed his forehead. That was it—they felt like equals.

She was glad he'd set his doubts aside about the baby. All of his *ifs* had stung her, no matter how much she'd tried to understand them. She ran her fingers lightly down the side of his cheek, studying every shadowy angle. He'd said he'd been *flame-thrower burned* in the past. What happened? She felt a wave of anger on his behalf. Hopefully he'd tell her someday.

Her fingers continued their journey across his shoulder, then down his chiseled chest. His mouth curved into a smile, even though his eyes remained closed.

"If you want to do that again, you need to let me recover, woman."

She trailed her fingers lower, following the trail that led below his stomach, which tightened at her touch.

"Oh, I want to do it again. I…um…*crave* you right now."

His eyes swept open, gazing straight into hers with a heat that made her burn with desire.

"You crave me, eh?" He took her by the waist and

slid her on top of him. "Well, I'm kind of tired, but if you're willing to do the work…"

Jade moved against him, and felt him begin to harden beneath her. Their bodies knew each other so well. She settled down over him, taking him in with a sigh. She really had been craving this feeling again. Trent reached up and cupped her breasts, massaging and teasing as she moved up and down. Her fire was beginning to build when he pressed one hand between her legs, using his fingers to…*oh my*…

Jade gave a cry, and hardly noticed when he scooped her into his arms and moved on top of her, taking her again until they both cried out this time. Trent slid off of her, lying on his back with one arm thrown over his face. She put her hand on her chest, just to be sure her heart was still in there, doing its job.

"Wow." She breathed the word more than spoke it.

He huffed out a low laugh.

"Yup."

The alarm on her phone woke them both a few hours later. Jade stretched and groaned as she reached for it. It wasn't in its usual spot on the bedside table. She sat up, then heard Trent muttering curse words under the blankets. Oh, yeah. Her phone was probably still in her pants pocket. Where had her pants ended up? On the floor somewhere. She got out of bed and found them, finally silencing the alarm.

"Sorry," she whispered to Trent. "Baker's hours are tougher than lawyer's hours."

His head popped up from beneath the covers, his eyes squinting from the bedroom light she'd turned on.

"What time is it?" His voice was gravelly and rough. A shock of dark blond hair fell over his forehead. He sounded and looked delicious. But she needed to shower and get to work. Today was baklava day.

"It's four thirty," she answered. He groaned and she just shrugged in response. "Today's an early day—I'm on my own in the kitchen until six when Joe arrives. Go back to sleep."

He didn't answer, and she thought he'd followed her advice. She tried to be as quiet as possible, closing the door to the small master bathroom. The whole room, floor to ceiling, was white marble. She stepped into the rainwater shower. It was nice, but with her schedule she sometimes wished for something with a little more force behind it. Something like a fire hose. She was rinsing her hair when she felt a cool draft come across her skin from behind. Then a warm body made up for it, stepping under the water with her. She dropped her head back against Trent's chest.

"I thought you were going back to sleep?"

"Once I knew you were in here naked and wet? Not likely. Here, let me help with that." He took her hair and held it under the water, then pressed a kiss against the back of her neck. "Do we have time for more than a shower? I know you need to get to work."

There was something surprisingly sweet about him not pressing for shower sex when she had work to do. Because as much as she *wanted* shower sex, he was right. She needed to get to the bakery.

"Can we put shower sex on hold until later? I'm sorry, but…"

"Don't be sorry." He took a washcloth and scrubbed her back, then turned her around and did the same to her front, being extra gentle around Bunny. "We're both adults, Jade. And 'later' means you see us doing this again." He cupped the side of her face with his hand. "Mind if I come watch you work? I'm wide awake and the rest of the world isn't, so…"

She nodded, stepping around him to exit the shower. "I'd like that. Use the back door—it'll be locked, but just knock and I'll let you in. I might even cook you breakfast."

He pulled her back in the shower for a quick kiss. "You bake. *I'll* make breakfast."

Her smile stayed on her face all the way to the bakery kitchen. Even though it was a raw, rainy November morning. Even though she'd lost precious hours of sleep last night. None of that mattered for some reason. Well, for a *Trent* reason. Was it smart to bring him this far into her life? She wasn't sure. But she couldn't imagine turning him away.

Because she was falling for him. And not just because he was the father of her daughter. She had a feeling she'd have fallen for Trent *without* Bunny.

Trent checked his watch and laughed to himself. Who'd have ever thought he'd be up, dressed and *happy* about it at five in the morning? But for over two weeks now, he'd been joining Jade nearly every morning in the kitchen at The Sweet Greek Bakery. Most of those mornings, he walked down from her apartment to the kitchen with her. Once in a while they'd stay at the hotel…since he was still paying for it…and he'd drive her into town in the predawn darkness. Today was the second day in a row where there'd been snow on the ground. Not a lot, but enough to make things bright and fresh whenever the sun finally rose.

From the beginning, they'd agreed to take things one day at a time, no pressure, no obligations, no strings. They could have sex and enjoy each other's company without getting serious. But things were feeling a lot more serious now that weeks had gone by.

Jade and Joe were busy putting together big sheets of baklava. Joe's wife, Pat, was mixing cookie dough in the commercial mixer. Trent had offered to help more than once, but after a few attempts, the *real* bakers had relegated him to his corner perch with firm orders not to touch anything. He could grill a

mean steak, and he knew how to make mouthwater-
ing chili. He could cook up enough pulled pork to
feed a crowd. He was a breakfast *beast*. But baking
had never been his thing, and he was smart enough
to admit it. At least, he'd admitted it after Jade told
him so.

It was his job to make sure there was coffee ready
in back for the bakers. They also gave him permission to prepare the hot water dispensers for the tea
counter out front, and he was getting good at select-
ing a different variety of teas for each day. He was
even beginning to enjoy drinking a few of the teas,
although he was definitely more of a coffee guy.

And this week, Jade had even trusted him with
the computer, giving him access to the spreadsheets
and allowing him to enter some of the bookkeeping
numbers...but only if she was able to check his work
afterward. She was the Woman in Control. He respected that. It was hot.

He watched her bending over the worktable,
brushing each sheet of phyllo dough with butter, and
sprinkling every third sheet with finely chopped pis-
tachios mixed with cinnamon and sugar. Her hair
was pulled into a knot high on her head. Her face
was a study in concentration.

A few hours earlier, she'd been concentrating on
something else entirely. She'd been sending him right
off the edge of sanity with her magical mouth, finally
making him yell so loudly he was afraid the sound

might make it through the thick brick walls of her apartment to the one next door. When he mentioned it later, she'd just laughed. "Benjamin's twenty-three and walked himself into an 'at your age' conversation a while back. I don't mind him knowing there's no age limit on orgasms."

They'd lain in each other's arms after that, talking as they often did just before the alarm went off. It turned out Trent didn't mind going to bed early. Not when he was going to bed with Jade. And they both had natural body clocks and tended to wake up right around the time the alarm was set for.

She'd heard from her father the day before, and she'd been distracted and withdrawn.

"Still mad about your dad's call?" he'd whispered, his arms wrapped around her, with her back to his chest. Spooning was their favorite thing to do after sex.

"More disappointed than mad. I'd really hoped he'd make it for Thanksgiving next week, but Marla conveniently made plans for them to go to my half sister's new house. Because they just moved in and Marla thought they should support them as they started out. As if *I* didn't just move. As if *I'm* not starting out, too. While *pregnant*."

"Hmm," Trent had replied, nuzzling her neck. "You sound mad to me."

She'd laughed softly. "Maybe a little. And Ashley *did* invite me to come, too. I don't like competing with my half sister, but it feels like everything with us becomes a competition anyway. It's exhausting. And now Marla's all ticked off because I'm having the first grandchild. I mean, I'm thirty-five. It's about time I had a kid, don't you think?"

At that point, he'd rolled her onto her back and grinned down at her. "Yeah, you're definitely mad. I'm sorry they're not coming, but *I'm* here, and we've been invited to Blake and Amanda's for Thanksgiving dinner. It sounds like there'll be a crowd there, so maybe that will help put a smile on your face." The Randalls said they liked opening up their home during holidays for anyone who wasn't traveling or having a houseful of company themselves.

Jade and Joe high-fived each other in the kitchen. The baklava was in the oven. The honey and rosewater syrup was already prepared, waiting to be poured over the hot, flaky pastry when it came out. She scrubbed her hands, then walked over to where Trent was sitting. He handed her a decaf coffee. She held it out to the side, stepped between his legs and leaned in for a kiss. He was more than happy to oblige.

"Mmmm," Jade sighed. "I like having you here in the mornings. As long as you don't bake."

He traced kisses down her neck, smiling against her warm skin. "I drop one lousy bag of flour and I get banned for life."

"It was a twenty-five-pound bag. And you knocked over a stack of egg cartons with it. It took all day to clean up the gooey mess." She moved her head back so he had easier access to her neck.

"You're a tough boss. One mistake and…"

"One? Are you forgetting the three trays of burnt cookies you were supposed to take out of the ovens after fifteen minutes? Or the actual cream you put in the snickerdoodle cookie dough instead of cream of tartar?" She pulled back, resting in the circle of his arms around her waist. She took a sip of coffee and flashed a quick smile. "Dude, you *suck* at baking." She gave him a swift kiss. "But you're really good at other things, which is why I like having you around."

They'd settled into an easy banter. Snarky, sly, clever…whatever it was, it worked for them. They instinctively knew that neither was trying to cause pain with their sarcasm. They respected each other too much for that. They cared too much. They loved… Trent gave himself a mental shake. He couldn't go there yet. You couldn't fall in love with someone this quickly…or this easily. That didn't happen in real life.

Jade took another big sip of coffee, her eyes closing in bliss. Damn, she was turning him on just by drinking coffee! But that wasn't love. Yes, they'd clearly had insta-lust at the wedding. But insta-*love*? He wasn't sure he believed in love at all, much less the instant kind. And yet he felt something for her. And it was a hell of a lot more than just friendship. Or just sex.

And that was a problem, because he'd permanently sworn off serious relationships. He wasn't built for them. No one in his family was.

But he couldn't imagine *not* having Jade Malone standing in his arms like this every morning, dusted with flour and sugar, turning him on with a sigh.

Chapter Thirteen

Trent and Jade left Halcyon after a delicious Thanksgiving dinner and hours of laughter with their friends. He looked over to where Jade had already nodded off in the passenger seat. They were in Trent's SUV. His *actual* SUV, which he'd driven back to Gallant Lake the previous weekend after flying to Denver to start clearing his apartment. He was narrowing down his job options here, and he knew he wasn't going back to Colorado. So he'd given his notice to the landlord and hired movers.

His sister, Sylvie, had agreed to oversee the rest of the move on that end. They'd had their ups and downs through the years, but they'd weathered their parents' multiple divorces together, which created a unique sibling bond. She'd told Trent she was excited that he was making a fresh start away from Denver.

Sylvie had separated from her husband, again, last year. Typical Michaels marriage—unsuccessful. But she seemed in a better place this year, and even talked about giving her husband, Craig, yet another chance.

What Trent didn't know was exactly *how* his fresh start would happen. He had money set aside from when he and Cindy had sold their house in the divorce. Should he find a place for himself? Or should he and Jade find a place *together*? As direct as conversations could be between the two of them, they'd tap-danced around the topic of moving in together like they were on *Dancing With the Stars*.

They kept busy telling each other this was a one-day-at-a-time thing. Totally casual. But it was feeling more permanent—more *solid*—every day. Hell, they'd just had their first Thanksgiving dinner together, like a real couple.

Jade had started house-hunting with local agent Brittany Thomas. She said she was looking for a rental house for herself, but Trent had been tagging along. For now, the official plan was that he'd take the apartment for the rest of her lease, since the place wasn't pregnancy or child friendly. But considering he was spending every night with Jade, that plan was subject to change. If they ever talked about it.

Her eyes swept open when he parked the car, and

she stretched. "It's pretty bad when I fall asleep on a five-minute drive."

"Hey…you're sleeping for two, right?" She waited for him to come around and open her door. He was making progress with her. She even reached for his arm. Or maybe she just needed his help. She sighed as she stood.

"Sorry—I'm also standing and walking for two. Except today it feels like three after eating that big meal. I can't imagine how I'm going to feel after another two months." She was due January twentieth.

"That's why you need to get out of this damn loft, Jade." They were at the bottom of the outdoor stairs. "Maybe we should've gone to my suite tonight."

"I'm fine." She brushed him off and headed up the stairs.

"Of course you are." Luckily she couldn't see him rolling his eyes at her backside. She was always *fine*. If a person could have a brand, that was hers.

They went into the apartment and she looked out the windows at the sunset. "Ugh. It's too early to go to bed, even for me. Want another beer?"

"No, I'll have a water with you. Go sit. I'll get it."

She sat on the sofa, swinging her feet up to put them in Trent's lap once he sat. It was another thing that had become routine. She loved his foot rubs, and he loved the little sounds she made while he rubbed her feet. It was a win-win. She dropped her head back against the pillow.

"Am I a terrible person for just assuming you want my puffy feet in your lap every night?"

He smiled as he started massaging her left foot. "I don't mind, so no, you're not terrible. I'm glad to help."

"And you know you'll get laid later, right?"

"Well, yeah—that, too."

After a few minutes of comfortable silence, she lifted her head to look at him. "Hey, did you talk to your family at all today to wish them a happy Thanksgiving?"

And…there went the comfortable vibe. He shook his head. "I called my dad last night, but he didn't pick up. My sister said he's in Mexico or somewhere for the weekend, so he may not have service." Or he may not want to talk to his only son. *Dad still hadn't forgiven him for changing his career path.* He took her other foot.

"But you talked to your sister?"

"Briefly, yeah. We just saw each other last weekend when I picked up my car."

Jade's head fell back against the pillows as he rubbed her foot. "I never asked—what does she think about you becoming a father? I'm assuming you told her?"

"Of course. There was stunned silence for a minute, then some, uh…questions."

"I'll bet. Who? What? When? Where?"

"Something like that, yeah." It was more like *What*

do you know about this woman? Are you sure it's yours? Real heartwarming stuff. "She wishes us both well and can't wait to meet the baby."

Jade was quiet so long he thought she'd fallen asleep. He gently rubbed the top of her feet, but it wasn't long before her eyes swept open again. "Ugh… I am so tired." Another pause. "You don't like talking about your family, do you?"

"Where did that question come from?" It was true, but why was she so hung up on *family* tonight?

"I don't know. Holidays. Baby on board. Turkey coma." She sat up with a mischievous grin, her feet still in his lap. "Indulge me, okay? I've told you all about my mom and stepmom and my dad and my grandmother and Ashley and all my jobs and most of my boyfriends." She was ticking off the topics on her fingers as she talked. "But you are still such a closed book. I know a little about your parents and sister and job, but the rest of your life is a blank slate."

He pinched her toe playfully, eager to distract her. "You make me sound like I was in prison or something. You know I went to school at UC Berkeley, majoring in environmental law. Then my dad browbeat me into going into good old reliable corporate law. I thought I was stuck there—" he pinched her toe again, making her jump "—until I met a mesmerizing woman at a wedding, knocked her up, and now I'm living my dream."

She giggled, but she didn't quit. "I'm pretty sure there was a marriage somewhere in there, too."

He went still. "You know there was. You also know I don't want to talk about it." He stared out the windows, where Gallant Lake was now dark. Jade waited, and he knew she'd wait as long as she needed to.

"Do we have to do this?" He shifted in his seat. "Cindy lied. She cheated. She broke my heart. End of story."

Jade knew she was pushing too hard. Today was Thanksgiving. She should give the guy a break. But it bothered her that he was holding back. That he was letting one relationship block all others.

Because she was falling in love with the man.

The realization sent her pulse rushing. She was in love with Trent. They'd spent all their nights together, having the intimate conversations people have when they're falling in love. Learning about each other. Sharing stories. Laughing over silly things they've done in the past. Or, like the other night, getting a hug from Trent while she cried over missing her mom more than ever now that she was getting ready to *be* a mother herself.

He'd been there for her. He cared. She'd seen it in his eyes not only when they were making love, but also when he sat in the bakery kitchen in the early mornings watching her work. She always knew when his eyes were on her, even when she wasn't facing him. She felt the heat.

But he kept saying how *bad* he was at relationships. How burned he'd been. And she needed to know more. So she waited. After a few minutes, Trent's shoulders fell and his gaze met hers.

"Cindy and I got married when we did because she said she was pregnant."

Jade took a sharp breath, stunned and saddened as the pieces began to fall into place. So many things made sense now. She reached over and took his hand, letting her feet drop to the floor.

"No wonder you didn't want to believe me." She spoke the thought out loud. "So you *do* have a child?" One that he'd never mentioned.

He gave an abrupt shake of his head. "No." A pause. "She insisted I not tell anyone she was pregnant until after the wedding. A week after our honeymoon, she told me she'd lost the pregnancy." Trent's jaw moved back and forth, a muscle ticking in his cheek. "That's just how she said it—she *lost the pregnancy*. Not *that she'd lost our child*."

"You don't think she was ever pregnant." Jade had never once thought of Bunny as a pregnancy.

"At the end, when we were just hurting each other for sport with our words, she told me she'd never been pregnant at all." He stared at the floor. "I really have no idea what was true and what wasn't. She had such a loose relationship with the truth that she may not have known anymore."

Silence hung over them. It was tense at first, pulsating with the pain and anger Trent still carried. But as Jade snuggled closer to him, lending her warmth and love, the tension began to ease. They'd cleared a hurdle. He'd told her at least some of the story.

She could see herself having a life with this man. A good life. She just wanted to know what she was up against when it came to baggage. And now she had a pretty good idea. It was daunting, but she could deal with a challenge she knew about. She didn't want to ruin this giant step forward by pushing him further than he was ready to go.

"Let's go upstairs, babe," she whispered. "I'm beat."

He turned to her, his face lined with regret. "I know you want to hear more. And there *is* more. I just…that's not my happy place." He eased himself to his feet, bringing her with him. She slid into his embrace, and he welcomed her with a gentle smile. "I don't want to spend time there. *You* make me happy, though. And I'd love to spend more time with you." His gaze grew serious. "A *lot* more time."

Her heart fluttered inside her chest. Was he suggesting getting serious? Or at least—officially serious? She had a feeling their hearts were already there. They were spending every night together.

Things were good—*really* good. She moved closer, looking straight into his eyes.

"Why don't we look for a place where we can both live? Together. With our daughter." She touched his face with her fingers. "Trent… I'm falling in love with you."

She hadn't really planned on blurting that out, but it was the truth, and he was a man who valued the truth more than most. He didn't react the way she'd hoped, though. He didn't react at all. Finally he cleared his throat and seemed to compose himself.

"You shouldn't." He couldn't look directly at her. She held her breath, not sure what he was saying. "My marriage did something that… Well, it makes it hard for me to let that word land on my heart in any way other than pain." He rushed to continue when he saw her face. "I care about you. I'm falling, but I can't define where I'm falling to, if that makes any sense. I care about what we have together. I'm just not in a place to answer with the same…"

"Trent." She put her finger against his lips, recognizing panic when she saw it. "I didn't say that as a ploy to get you to say it back to me." Although it would have been nice to hear. "I just thought you should know that I'm in love with you." She removed her finger from his mouth and kissed him softly. "It's okay if you need more time."

It wasn't okay. Not really. His refusal to accept her love hurt. His insistence that his first marriage had rendered him unlovable made her angry with the woman who'd convinced him of that. But she could see the pain and fear in his eyes, and she didn't want to end a good day on a sour note.

She turned and pulled him along with her. "Let's get some sleep. The tryptophan from all that turkey is making us both loopy."

Things were strained over the next week. Not as if they'd argued or anything. But Jade felt Trent begin to withdraw the moment she'd said she loved him. Whoever that Cindy lady was, Jade would really like to have a chat with her. In a dark alley somewhere. With a baseball bat in her hand.

She blinked and straightened, looking around the bakery kitchen as if someone might have heard her dreamed-up scenario out loud. She wasn't the violent sort. But then again, at her current hormone levels, she might just be capable of anything. Particularly against the woman who'd damaged Trent so badly.

He was her calm and steady rock, and he had been right from the first night they'd met. But he was hiding a pain that ran really deep. So deep that he didn't want to admit his true feelings for her. Because she was very sure he was falling right along with her. They were on the same page, but he was fighting it—flailing around and stomping his feet trying to deny it.

She smiled as she got up to check the turnovers in

the ovens. She could be patient. They'd looked at a few houses with Brittany and she had a feeling he was silently agreeing they should live together.

But every house had something that one of them didn't like. Too big. Too small. No yard. Busy road. Owners wanted to sell instead of rent. She dismissed the nagging thought that their lack of commitment to a house might be a sign of something that needed to be dealt with sooner rather than later.

She turned off the ovens and pulled the turnovers out, leaving them to cool. The bell chimed out front, and she hurried to greet the customer. She was on her own today, with Joe and Pat taking a much-deserved day off. After the holidays, they'd be running the store full-time through her maternity leave, with some part-time help from a few locals she'd managed to line up for those months. The business was doing well. Well enough that she was feeling a lot better about it surviving without her constant presence.

The customer was reading the community bulletin board near the counter, but Jade recognized his profile right away.

"*Anthony?* Oh my God, what are you doing here?" She came around the counter to hug her former head chef. They'd formed not only a great partnership in the high-stress environment of a busy, upscale kitchen back in St. Louis, but they'd become friends, too.

Anthony embraced her, then held her shoulders

as he stepped back to look at her stomach. "So the rumors are true? You're expecting a little sous-chef soon?"

"It'll be a few years before she can help in the kitchen, I'm afraid." She gestured at the display case. "What would you like to try? Pour yourself some tea and we can catch up. And the first thing I want to know is what the hell you're doing in my bakery."

"I want to try everything I see, Jade. This all looks amazing, which is no surprise, knowing your pastry skills. How about a kunafa nest and a slice of that baklava?" He poured two teas while she pulled out the pastries. "I'm assuming you want decaf?" She nodded, then joined him at a table by the window. He took a bite of baklava and sighed. "You used rose water *and* orange blossom water, didn't you? It's perfect. As far as how I got here, I ran into your dad last month and he said you opened your own place in some God-forsaken town called Gallant Lake." He gave a one-shoulder shrug. "I'm interviewing at a new restaurant in lower Manhattan, so I had to drive up here and see if it was true." He looked around the shop. "It's beautiful. And *you're* beautiful, Jade."

Behind him, Trent walked into the bakery just as he said that. Trent's smile quickly went from bright to brittle. She stood to greet him, but his eyes were on Anthony.

"Anthony, this is..." How was she supposed to introduce him? Her *casual* boyfriend? Her baby daddy? The man she loved but who didn't want her to say so? She cleared her throat. "This is Trent Michaels. He's the father of my little future chef. Trent, this is Anthony Beaumont. He and I ran the restaurant kitchen together back in St. Louis."

Anthony scrambled to his feet, taking Trent's hand, then folding him into an embrace. Anthony was a hugger. Trent did not return it. Anthony clapped Trent on the back. "Congratulations, my friend! You got the best pastry chef in the Midwest in this girl. And the prettiest, too! I always said she had the looks of a Greek goddess. My Mediterranean queen."

There was a tightness around Trent's eyes that Jade couldn't decipher. Was he angry? Maybe a job prospect hadn't gone well. He'd had a few interviews that didn't pan out—they wanted him in a physical office too often, or they couldn't afford to pay him enough, or their approach to protecting the environment didn't quite align with his. She supported his decision to find the best fit possible. He'd told her he had enough money set aside to be able to take his time...to a point.

Trent stared at her. "I didn't think Jade was the type who wanted to be worshiped, but maybe I was wrong."

She rolled her eyes. "Please—old-fashioned chivalry is wasted on me."

"Anthony doesn't seem to think so."

Anthony laughed, but Jade picked up on the slight edge in Trent's voice. Was he... *jealous*? She'd never seen him act possessive before, but it's not like they'd known each other all that long. Then she remembered—he'd said his ex Cindy had cheated on him.

She went to the counter to get Trent a pastry, then returned to the table, where he was now chatting with Anthony as if they were pals. She wondered if she'd imagined everything, but no. There was still a chill in his eyes, and he kept looking back and forth between Anthony and her. It wasn't enough for Anthony to notice, but it was there.

After her old friend left to head back to Manhattan, with a promise to stop by another time when he could stay longer, Jade turned to Trent, her hands on her hips.

"You *do* know Anthony is gay, right? There was no need for that green streak I saw."

A flash of surprise crossed his face, then his expression changed to innocence. "I don't care about his sexual orientation, Jade. And what green streak?"

"Right." She turned away to cash out the register and get ready to close the shop. "I know jealousy when I see it, and it's ridiculous. We were just friends and former co-workers. Even if we *were* wild lovers in the past, why would you care? You're the one who keeps telling me we're not serious."

And there it was. Her frustration with Trent's resistance had finally surfaced. His continued denial of what they had together was grating on her nerves. Enough already.

Heavy silence fell on the shop. Bunny kicked her hard, and she put her hand on the side of her stomach and pushed back gently, then she led Trent back to the kitchen.

"You need to decide what you want from me. From *us*." She stopped next to the big ovens and spread her hands wide. "What are we *doing*? You keep insisting we're casual, but then you turn around and go house hunting with me. You get jealous. We're together every night." She was ticking off each point on her fingers. "You're moving to Gallant Lake. I told you I *love* you. And you just keep saying *nope* to us. To a real life together. To a relationship. To *me*."

She flattened her hand on her chest, suddenly realizing where her hurt was coming from. She'd felt such a sense of *belonging* with Trent. But what if he wasn't just scared? What if he really didn't feel the same way? What if he didn't *want* her in his life long term, other than as the mother of his child? Was she destined to be an outsider with Trent, too?

He jammed his fingers through his thick, sandy hair and stared up at the ceiling, his fingers locked together on top of his head. "I'm sorry. I don't know what fired me off..." He dropped his hands and looked at her. "That's not true. I *do* know. I had a call from dear old Dad this morning and it put me in a mood. I came to talk to you about it and this guy

I've never seen is gushing all over you and calling you his queen, and it was like salt in a fresh wound." He ran his fingers absently along the edge of the baking table where she and Joe had made baklava that morning. "I came here today looking for a friendly shoulder, Jade. I don't care about that Anthony guy."

A friendly shoulder. How romantic. How...*casual*. She frowned. Maybe she'd read more into his feelings than was actually there. It wasn't like he hadn't tried to tell her he didn't want a relationship. She took a deep breath.

"Apology accepted. But I'm not your emotional punching bag. If you want to talk about something, fine. But you don't get to throw that crap at me like a weapon." He nodded in agreement, still looking troubled. Damn it, she couldn't just stop caring about the man. "What did your dad say that upset you so much?"

He sat at the desk by the back door. He handed her a bottle of water from the nearby cooler as she joined him, sitting on the desk. Trent was constantly making sure she was hydrated. She waited until he was ready to talk.

"He was agitated. Maybe he'd started his morning with a few too many bloody Marys." He gave her a slanted smile. "Speaking of punching bags, I think he's missing *his*, which was me. He told me what a mistake it was to leave a steady job for uncertainty, leave big money for environmental pennies, and on and on." He shrugged. "And, of course, he had to give me his opinion about you and me and the baby and my failed marriage and how gullible I am…" His voice trailed off, but she heard the hurt in it.

"And then you found me giggling away with a good-looking man from my past." She paused. "I'm beginning to understand where your doubts came from, but that doesn't make them okay, Trent. You *have* to start trusting me. We're going to be parents together."

He nodded, staring at the desk. "I know. But…" He waited a beat before continuing. "That stuff might come up once in a while, whether you deserve it or not. I told you I'm bad at relationships, babe. My whole family is wired to think everyone's out to screw us over. Dad's father raised *him* to believe it, and he raised Sylvie and I to have the same skeptical outlook. Add in a few experiences where people actually *did* screw us over, and…" He finally looked up at her. "And we're all just suspicious as hell."

"Yeah, I've noticed."

He huffed out a low laugh. "I'll do my best, okay? And as far as the *casual* business goes, I think we both know we've moved past casual. How far, I don't know."

She moved from the chair to his lap, sliding her arms around his neck, needing to be close to him.

"Well, I told you I'm in love with you, so *I'm* in this pretty far."

He nodded, his mouth a grim line. He rested his forehead against hers, and she could feel him fighting with himself.

"I know, Jade. I just… I can't go there yet."

"Will you ever?" she whispered, stuck somewhere between hope and dread.

He looked at her through his thick, honey-colored eyelashes. "I'm trying, babe. I promise you that much. I'm trying."

They left it at that, sealed with a quick kiss before they closed up the kitchen and walked back to her place with an unspoken agreement to let the subject go.

She knew *trying* was the best he could give her right now. All she had to do was decide if *trying* was enough for her, and for how long.

Chapter Fourteen

Trent threw his phone onto the sofa and started pacing again. He'd been on edge since Dad's call last week, doing his best to ignore the jabs that always seemed to find their mark. That Jade was trying to entrap him. That he was throwing away his career—hell, his whole life. That moving to the Catskills would never make him happy. That he'd come crawling back to Denver eventually, poorer and weaker than ever.

Jade had managed to talk him down on Thursday, but now it was Monday afternoon and Dad's call was *still* on replay in his mind. Add in the call he'd just finished with his sister, and he could feel the walls closing in on him. He *was* making a mistake.

And the mistake was falling in love with Jade Malone.

There was nothing he could do about the falling in love part. That was a done deal. He may not have said the words yet, but they were already branded on his heart. He loved her. That made him vulnerable. And even worse, it made *her* vulnerable. Vulnerable to his doubts. His suspicions. His inability to tell her things. He was just like his father, which meant that every relationship he touched ended up imploding on itself, leaving people wounded in the aftermath. He could take the hit. But he'd be damned if he could let Jade be hurt.

Not by him.

He poured his second shot of scotch and gulped it down. Jade was shopping with Amanda and Nora. They'd gone to White Plains to check out nursery furniture, even though there was no nursery yet, and no house to put one in. They'd seen a bunch of houses, including one rambling contemporary ranch over near the ski lodge that they'd both liked a lot. The owners wanted to sell, but Brittany thought she could talk them into a limited lease.

Now Trent was wondering if they should do *anything* together. Not that he wouldn't help pay for it, since she was having his child and he *did* love Jade. He wanted her—*needed* her—to be happy. But living together?

If the best he could hope for was a roller coaster

of an on again/off again marriage like Sylvie's, or a revolving door like Dad's, then Jade would be better off without him. He didn't *want* to hurt her, but better to hurt her now than let her *really* fall in love with him before she discovered the truth—that he wasn't wired for happy relationships. Sure, they were having fun now, but how long could that possibly last?

At the very least, they needed to slow things down. Preferably to a complete halt. Before he had a chance to totally mess up her life.

He was still thinking about how to break it to her when Jade got back to the apartment later that night.

She shrugged off her coat and nodded at the glass in his hand. "Bad day?"

He took another swallow of the liquid courage, then cleared his throat as the whiskey burned its way down the inside of his chest.

"We need to talk."

Jade's smile faded. "O-kay. Has something happened?"

Sylvie's phone call had pushed Trent to face the facts once and for all. This relationship had been doomed from the start. He took a deep breath.

"I don't want there to be any misunderstanding about what we're doing. We said *no strings* that first night at the wedding, and we said it again when we started sleeping together here in Gallant Lake—"

Her right brow arched high. "And almost every night since then."

"Yeah…that was probably a mistake." He winced, knowing that no matter how true it was, it was the wrong thing to say.

"*Excuse* me?" She sat up straight on the edge of her chair. "Did you just say *mistake*? To describe *us*?"

"There shouldn't even *be* an us, Jade. *That's* the mistake. That doesn't mean it wasn't great…um… physically—"

"Oh, gee. Thanks." Her eyes clouded with hurt and anger. "And as far as that whole *no strings* BS from our first night?" She patted her stomach, which was growing all the time. "Bunny would like a word. There are endless strings now." Her brows lowered. "Wait, are you doubting she's yours again? Come on, Trent. I can't have this conversation every time you have a panic attack, or pity party, or whatever this is. This baby is *yours*."

"I know that. This isn't about that." She started to speak, but her mouth snapped shut as he talked over her, desperate to explain his jumbled feelings. "It's not a *you* problem. It's *me*. I don't trust my own judgment. It's *me* I'm doubting. My ability to be her father. I'll give it everything I've got, but to be any more than that…*that's* what I'm saying I don't think I can do."

Her face fell. "What are you talking about? You said you'd try…"

"I've said a lot of things, Jade." His voice hard-

ened with the determination to get this over with.
Rip off the bandage. "Things have moved fast. I've
made decisions that maybe I shouldn't have. And
now I think it's time to dial things back, before we...
go too far."

He watched as each word struck her heart. But
this had to be done. He'd made the mistake of falling in *love*, which was the one thing he swore he'd
never do again. He'd screwed it up so badly the first
time, and now he was doing it all over again. Which
proved he was right to stop this *now*, before it got
any worse.

"Look, you don't *want* me to be with you—trust
me. You've seen it—I'm too closed up. I'm jealous.
I'm insecure. I'm just plain *bad* at keeping people
in my life. They always leave. I couldn't live with
myself if I hurt *you*. And I can't afford to lose my
daughter."

"*Lose* her?" Jade's hand went to her stomach
again. "What the *hell* are you talking about?"

He tried to come up with the right words, but
he couldn't describe his fear. He drained his glass.
Maybe that meant his fear was absurd, but...that
didn't change the fact that it existed. And since he'd
arrived in Gallant Lake, the fear of impending disaster had grown until it began to consume him.

"I don't mean any harm would come to her. I
meant losing her from my life. That would...that
would break me."

"Trent…" She reached out to take his hand, now clenched on his knee. He wouldn't open his fingers, so she held his wrist instead. Her fingers touched on his pulse, and he could have sworn his heart skipped a few beats. "You're not making sense. Why do you think you'd lose her? I'd never keep her from you. We have an agreement…"

He gave a harsh laugh. "We have a casual custody agreement between two people who are sleeping together. Once we're married, it's a whole different ball game."

She released him as if his skin was burning her, her eyes narrowing. "I don't recall receiving a marriage proposal from you."

"I know that." Beads of sweat gathered on his back, some trickling a path downward. The same direction his hope was traveling. "I… I'm just saying that if we get serious and things fall apart, then…you could take her away or…something. I don't know—"

Jade sat back, putting ever more distance between them. "Did you just say *if* we get serious? You don't think we're *already* serious?"

There was a long beat of heavy silence.

"I'm saying we can't get any *more* serious. You may not like the word, but it was a mistake for me to let it go this far. The idea of becoming a father made me lose my head, but I know how this ends. I don't want that for either one of us, but I especially don't want it for you."

Jade stood, using that familiar rocking motion she'd picked up over the past few weeks to get to her feet while balancing the baby. She started pacing the floor, stopping to absently adjust the tinsel garland in the apartment windows. Christmas would be here in another week or two.

"I thought things were good—like *really* good between us. I thought we were becoming a family. That we were…" She turned to face him. "That we were in *love*. We *are* in love with each other, Trent." She pointed her finger at him. "I *love* you. And you love me, too. I know it. I *know* it." She came back and sat again. "You're just having a panic attack right now. It's normal. There's been a lot of changes and—"

"I'm thirty-eight years old." Trent shook his head, refusing to let her logic deter him. "This isn't *panic*, Jade. It's *experience*. Wisdom. I know myself, and I know what I'm capable of. I've been down this road before."

A slideshow of memories flipped through his mind. Coming home after an overnight business trip to Nevada. Opening the front door to a house holding nothing but his few personal possessions and a closet full of suits and ties. The furniture was gone. Pictures gone off the walls. Cindy must have hired movers to have emptied it so fast.

He could still hear the echo of his footsteps as he wandered from room to room in disbelief. The desolation of standing in Harper's room, with its cheery pink walls and star decals on the ceiling. The giant unicorn wall stickers. The empty closet. The only tangible thing left in the room was a tiny pink feather boa with glitter on it—a gift he'd given Harper on her fifth birthday. Discarded on their way out of his life. He blinked away the memory of the crushing sense of failure he'd felt that night.

"Jade, you have to believe that I never meant to hurt you and I've let this go too far." His words tumbled out, stumbling over each other. "That's on me. I want us to be friends so we can co-parent efficiently, but going further than being friends just won't work. It's too big a risk, and one that won't pay off in the long run, so I think it's most prudent to just—"

"Oh. My. God." Her dark eyes went as hard as onyx. "Did that word salad you just spewed really say it's you, not me, that you want to be friends, *and* include lawyeresque words like *efficiently* and *prudent*?" He didn't answer, getting her point but not wanting to acknowledge it. She stared at him for a moment, then looked down at the floor, her forehead furrowed. "You need to go."

He shook his head. "We should talk this through. Come to an agreement…"

"Did you hear me?" Her expression was stony when you looked up. "You need to go. As in *get out*. Leave my presence. Don't let the door hit you on the ass on your way out. Go away. Shoo." She pointed at the door. "Can I make it any more clear?"

"I'm not leaving until we resolve—"

"You don't set the rules here. You especially don't set them for *me*." She pushed up to her feet again, and he stood to help her, but she slapped his hand away. "If this is really the way you want things, then I guess we *should both hire attorneys*. Maybe *they'll* be friends. So go away. This pregnancy is officially none of your business, because *I'm* the one who's pregnant, and you don't want to be part of my life. Once I deliver, our attorneys can work out a visitation schedule for you to see your daughter."

Trent scrubbed his hands down his face again and let out a loud growl of frustration. Maybe the liquid courage hadn't been such a great idea, because he'd made a mess of what was supposed to be a calm, reasonable conversation.

"That's not the way I want this to play out. I *do* want to be part of your life. Part of *Bunny's* life. But not as…" He swallowed hard, forcing his voice to stay steady. "Not as some sort of family unit. I'm doing you a favor, here." His frustration nearly choked him. "Family isn't in my DNA. I'll eventually screw up and destroy everything. Don't you get that?"

She folded her arms, her expression stony. "I'm beginning to, yeah. Because that's what you just did. You screwed up. And you did it as some sort of preemptive strike to avoid an *imagined* future. A vision that has no basis in what we've shared over the past weeks."

"I'm trying to protect you—"

"Bull," she scoffed. "You're protecting *yourself*. You're picking up your toys and going home. So stop talking about it and just…go." She looked away. "Please."

The last word came out as a near-whisper, her voice cracking. Her eyes were shining with tears that hadn't yet spilled over.

"I'll go, but I want you to think about what I—"

"I don't need to think about it. As you so tenderly put it, we are not going to be a *family unit*. So go live your life and I'll call you when Bunny is born so you can schedule a time to see her."

"That's not what I want—"

Her jaw tightened. "If you insist on denying your love for me, you will *not* be a part of my life. You can lie to yourself, but you can't lie to me. I won't put up with it." She jerked her head toward the door. "Goodbye, Trent."

Retreat was probably the best idea. Give her time to see that he was right. He went to the door. She'd done exactly what he'd been fearing the most—she'd cut him out of his life. He turned to find her watching him leave. She shook her head sadly at the far end of the hallway.

"I love you, Trent, but I don't have the energy or desire to raise *two* children. I can't hold your hand

and tell you why you're wrong about us. And I can't be constantly worrying about you bailing on me or on Bunny."

"I would *never* do that."

Her eyes softened, filled with sorrow.

"You just did."

Jade managed to smile at customers throughout the next day, even as she carried the cold weight of her broken heart inside her chest. Trent had blind-sided her last night, and she was struggling with how to move forward. Was it her declaration of love that chased him away? Was he still jealous about Anthony, even though she'd explained everything? Was the impending birth freaking him out? Or had he always planned on *being friends*?

She had a hard time believing that when she thought of their time together in her bedroom, or even just curled up in the living room together to watch a movie. Their connection had felt so real... so perfect. How could it *not* be love?

She made it through the day, but she knew her friends had noticed something was off. So she wasn't surprised on Wednesday, when Amanda showed up with Julie and Cassie from the resort, at lunchtime, insisting that Jade join them.

She looked back into the kitchen and caught Pat's eye, then agreed. She needed to give Pat more time at the counter anyway. The shop would be fine during her maternity leave. The only gaping hole in Jade's plan was the spot where Trent was supposed to be.

She took a piece of baugatsa for herself, pouring a cup of lavender mint tea and joining the ladies at a table. Julie studied her for a minute.

"Are you okay? You look a little—I don't know—tired? Sick? In pain?"

Cassie and Amanda joined Julie's intense examination of Jade. Amanda nodded. "Once I hit my eighth month with Maddy, my energy evaporated. It might be time for you to cut back your working hours."

Cassie, seated right next to her, leaned forward. "I don't think that's it, girls. She's been crying. What happened?"

"Nothing I want to talk about." Jade sipped her tea to avoid saying more. But this was Gallant Lake, and friends here didn't let that sort of comment fly.

"Want to or not, why don't you give it a try?" Julie asked gently.

She turned her tea mug back and forth on the table, replaying the conversation in her head for the hundredth time.

"Trent ended things Monday night."

There was a beat of silence as the other women exchanged stunned looks.

"What do you mean, sweetie?" Cassie leaned forward and took her hand.

"I mean he ended things. He said he doesn't want

to be a—and I'm quoting him here—a *family unit* with me." Her heart felt brittle inside her chest, as if the slightest touch would make it crumble.

"He's abandoning the baby?" Amanda's voice was breathless with shock. Jade shook her head with a short, humorless laugh.

"Not the baby. Just me." The weight of that statement felt like it would crush her. She looked up, determined not to give in to her heartbreak. At least not in public. "He wants to be in Bunny's life, but not me." Once again, she'd be the outsider.

"I don't understand." Julie shook her head. "I saw you two at Thanksgiving dinner. It was obvious to everyone that you were in love…"

"We were," Jade answered. "At least… *I* was. He said a bunch of nonsense about how he was doing me a *favor* because we were doomed to fail anyway. He said *family* wasn't in his DNA." Anger rose, choking her. "What does that even *mean*?"

"Was he still mad about your chef friend showing up?" Cassie asked.

"I think that may have started the spiral, but his dad got in his head, too. Trent told me he'd just ruin things eventually and insisted he was speaking from experience."

"Something had to have triggered such a drastic reaction." Cassie thought for a moment. "What do you know about his past?"

"Are you asking if he's a fugitive or something?"

Jade started to laugh, then sighed instead. "He doesn't like to talk about it, but he had a rough divorce." She frowned. "His parents divorced, too. And I think his sister?" Her voice hardened. "Maybe they're just a family of cut-and-run cowards."

Julie nodded in agreement. "Maybe they are." She looked around the table and shrugged. "What? Everyone here knows how the past can influence us years…hell, *decades* later. I almost ruined things with Quinn because of stuff that happened in my childhood that I couldn't get past. Amanda, you've faced those demons, too. And Cassie, it took a lot for you to trust Nick."

"And yet all three of you are happily married, so… what's the point?" Jade finished her tea and checked her watch. Half an hour until she could close up and go home to catch up on the sleep she didn't get last night. She'd tossed and turned, and her stress had gotten to Bunny, so even when Jade *did* start to nod off, Bunny would start kicking. She sat back. "I had a crappy childhood, too, but I'm fine." She stopped, knowing she'd just used a catchphrase her friends would recognize.

"*Are* you fine? Really?" Julie's words were soft. "Just because you say it all the time doesn't make it true. You left your family and friends behind and planted yourself in a town you'd never heard of before this year. You've opened your own business while being very pregnant. The father of your child is here messing with your head." Julie leaned forward. "*Are* you fine?"

Jade pinched her lips together tightly, chewing on the inside of her cheek. Of course she was fine. She was tough. She could do this. She pushed her chair back from the table.

"I was wrong about Trent and I, but hey, stuff happens, right?" She rose to her feet, which wasn't easy these days. "So yes, I'm fine. Or I will be."

Cassie gave her a pointed look. "Okay. You're fine. That's great. So here's the next question. Is *Trent* fine?"

Jade froze. "The guy who just broke up with me? Why should I care?"

The hurt he'd caused her laced through every word.

"Because you love him?" Amanda smiled softly.

She blinked, trying to breathe normally and failing. Her lungs were too tight with anger and betrayal to think about her love for him.

"I told him I loved him, and a few days later he played the *let's be friends* card on me. I don't know what more I can do. How could he think I'd take his daughter away from him?" Tears choked her voice. "So you know what? Screw him. I was going to do this alone anyway, so I'll go back to Plan A. He doesn't want to be a family with me and our daughter, anyway."

"I think that might be my fault." An unfamiliar voice spoke behind her. Jade turned to face the woman whose eyes matched Trent's. Her light brown hair was short and stylish. Her clothes were expensive—wool trousers and a suede jacket with a cashmere scarf. She tugged off leather gloves and held her hand out to Jade with a rueful smile. "I'm Sylvie Winstead. Sylvie *Michaels* Winstead. Trent's sister. And I'm pretty sure I'm the one who sent Trent on his latest cut-and-run." She closed her eyes and shook her head. "He's always been a scorched earth sort of guy—why fix something when you can just burn it to the ground to avoid facing it?" Her gaze landed on Jade again. "Can we talk? I don't mind sitting with your friends if you want the moral support, but I come in peace."

Amanda started to scoot her chair over to make room at the table. Cassie stopped her, offering her chair instead, saying she had to get back to work. Julie poured a cup of tea for Sylvie. Jade stood frozen in place, unsure how to react. But Sylvie had already accepted the tea *and* the seat at the table. It would be awkward to walk away without at least hearing her out. As hurt and angry as Jade was, she hadn't stopped loving Trent. She didn't imagine she ever would, no matter how much she wanted to.

Jade glanced at the counter, but Pat had things under control. She was already putting things away and getting ready for closing. Joe was doing the same in the kitchen. She sat back down.

Amanda made introductions, then got right to the point. "Tell us what's going on with your brother, Sylvie."

The woman, who looked to be in her forties, started to laugh. "How much time do we have?" She looked at Jade, then down to her baby bump, and her smile softened. "How are you? I mean, other than being pissed off at my little brother?"

Jade had no idea if she should trust Sylvie or not. Trent had barely mentioned her, but then again, he'd barely mentioned any of his family other than in generalities.

"I'm fine." She ignored the way Amanda and Julie rolled their eyes. "When did you arrive?" Trent hadn't mentioned any family visits.

"Just now." Pat brought over a plate of pastries and Sylvie took a bite of one. "Oh wow—he wasn't kidding about your baking skills. I caught a flight after talking to him Monday night, and no, Trent has no idea yet that I'm here. I stopped at the resort—which is gorgeous, by the way—and the desk clerk said he'd gone rock climbing with a friend. So I decided to come meet the woman who's about to make me an auntie. And who has put my brother in a tailspin."

"I did not—"

Sylvie held up her hand. "Oh, I know—you didn't force him to fall in love again. But he did, and then he hit panic city, right?"

Jade was beginning to suspect Sylvie was an ally.

She nodded in response. "Big time. I'm guessing you can help explain why?"

"Maybe," Sylvie answered, taking another nibble of her baklava. "Our father has been more of a loose cannon than usual lately. He and Trent never had a healthy relationship to begin with, and now that Trent has left Denver, Dad's been more…volatile. They've barely spoken to each other since Trent quit the law firm and went into what our dad calls 'hippy-dippy tree-hugger law.' But when we heard Trent had gotten someone…" She blushed when she glanced at Jade. "That he was going to be a father…well, Dad was convinced it was someone taking advantage, and he started emailing Trent a bunch of so-called legal advice. No offense."

Jade frowned into her teacup. "Offense *taken*, but not from you. Go on." Trent had never mentioned any emails from his father.

Sylvie winced. "Sorry. Our branch of the Michaels's family tree hasn't been able to make a marriage work in three generations. My aunt once said we were cursed, and I'm beginning to think she was on to something." She poured two packets of sugar into her tea, just like Trent.

"By the time the curse got to our generation, well…" She shrugged again. "Maybe it's a self-fulfilling prophecy—we look for relationships we know will fail. Or maybe we really are just that unlucky in love. Or *unable* to love, or unable to *remain* loveable by others." She held her finger against her nose, as if trying to stifle a sneeze…or tears. When she didn't continue, Julie spoke up.

"But what do you think triggered him yesterday? He was fine before that…well, other than that little jealousy thing…"

Jade frowned. His *little jealousy thing* had opened the door to this whole panic attack of his. His tension had been increasing over the past week or so…maybe because his father had been planting seeds of doubt?

"I swear it wasn't my intention to blow things up," Sylvie answered. "I told him Dad was filing for divorce from wife number four because he caught her cheating while they were on vacation. Apparently he caught her with a literal cabana boy in Mexico." She took a sip of tea. "Big shock, since she's only thirty years younger than he is. So Dad is redoing his will…again. He's been making a lot of dramatic noise about *disowning* Trent. I really think the problem is that Dad *misses* Trent and can't admit it. So he's being a big angry bear about everything."

Sylvie stopped for a sip of tea. "Our father is messing with Trent to get him to come back to Denver, where Dad can keep his thumb on him. I *told* Trent that, but I think I was too late. I could tell he was wound up." Her mouth twisted into a wry smile. "Then I told him my husband and I getting back together…again. This will be try number three for us, and Trent got *mad* about it. He said if I was smart, I'd walk away. It pissed me off, and…words were said. We argued and I knew he was going to do something stupid instead of just marrying you."

Jade's spoon clinked loudly on the edge of her cup. "What is up with all the marriage talk? Trent said something about marriage, but he's never mentioned it to me before. And now you're saying *you* talked to him about marrying me."

Sylvie's eyebrows rose high. "He hasn't *said* anything? But I mailed him the—" She stopped, her mouth pressed tightly closed.

"Mailed him what?" Jade demanded. "A ring or something?"

She looked at Jade, then slowly smiled. "Not a ring. Never mind. Maybe I misread the situation. Maybe that's why he got mad at me." She stopped again, then sighed. "No, that's not why. I was angry, and I blurted out that Cindy got married again." She looked at Amanda and Julie. "Cindy is his ex. I could tell I'd struck a nerve. He got really quiet."

Jade felt a chill across her skin, as if someone had just opened a window. Was Trent still in love with his ex? Was *that* why he'd never wanted to talk about her? Was that why he couldn't let himself fall in love with Jade?

"He still loves her?" She didn't want to know, but she *had* to know.

"Oh, *God* no," Sylvie snorted. "Not after what she did to him."

Jade tried to piece together the few times he'd mentioned Cindy. "He's only told me a little. She lied to him. She was unfaithful, right? And she left him?"

Sylvie's teacup was halfway to her mouth, and she froze. "Is that all he's told you?"

"What else is there?"

Sylvie was making it sound like Cindy was a secret serial killer. Sylvie set her cup down, her lips pursed together in thought.

"It's not my story to tell. And I know that might frustrate you, because my brother's so buttoned up about his feelings. All I'll say is Cindy is a big reason for that. None of us saw it coming, least of all Trent, but she ended up being…borderline abusive." She hesitated. "No, she *was* abusive, at least emotionally. She gaslighted him until he didn't know what was real and what wasn't. I told him Cindy sent Harper to live with her grandparents, which is honestly good news for the poor kid."

"Who's Harper?"

Sylvie frowned. "Cindy's daughter from one of her previous scams…er…relationships."

Jade blinked. "He had a stepdaughter?" He told her they didn't have a baby, but he'd never mentioned a stepdaughter.

"Oh, Trent," Sylvie breathed, "what have you done?" She put her hand on Jade's. "I can't believe he didn't tell you. Then again, it shouldn't surprise me. It's the Michaels way. He fell head over heels for

Cindy's little girl. Harper was four when they married, six when Cindy took her away. You should get the other details from Trent." She leaned forward. "Give him another chance, Jade. I could tell when he was in Denver before Thanksgiving that…" She cleared her throat. "Well, I could tell he was in love with you. I could hear it in his voice, in the way he laughed, and the way he opened up."

Too bad he hadn't opened up to *her*. At least things began to make more sense now.

If things fall apart you could take her away…

This isn't panic, Jade. It's experience…

I've been down this road before…

Trent had had a child—not *his* child, but a child he'd loved. And she'd been taken away from him forever. Another little piece of Jade's heart softened, but she stopped it right there. Yes, that was sad. She felt terrible that Trent had gone through it. But why hadn't he *told* her any of this? Just because it made sense didn't mean she had to forgive him.

"He told me that loving me was a mistake. That he'd destroy us. That he was doing me a favor by dumping me." Sylvie started to speak, but Jade talked over her. "I get that he may be damaged, and I'm sad for him, but…" She gestured at Bunny. "I'm a month away from having his baby. I won't keep her from him, but I can't let him into *my* life if he's not going to give me one hundred percent. I can't fix him and raise a baby and run a business. And frankly, I deserve a man who's not going to keep secrets from me, and who won't cut and run every time he feels a twinge of doubt coming on."

The table was silent, but she saw their agreement in the quiet nods. Even his sister seemed to understand that Trent would have to figure out how to grow up all by himself.

Chapter Fifteen

Trent opened the door to his suite and stared at his sister. He'd been expecting a pizza. Looking forward to it, even, after a long, difficult December rock climb with Nick that had ended with him being fiercely scolded by his friend for taking too many careless chances. He was *not* looking forward to the new lecture he could see waiting on his sister's lips. *Damn it.*

"I should have known." He stepped aside to let her into the room. There was no point in telling her to go away. "Come on in, Sylvie."

She glanced around the suite, then took a seat at the small table near the kitchenette. She hadn't had a chance to speak when the actual pizza arrived.

Good. Maybe that would keep her from speaking a while longer.

His sister watched as he grabbed a couple small plates, pulled two beers from the fridge, and joined her at the table. They ate their first slices in silence. Sylvie wasn't the silent type, so he knew she'd break eventually. But as usual between them, it turned into a competition. Story of their lives, thanks to their father constantly pitting them against each other since childhood.

It wasn't until after she'd finished her second slice that she finally spoke, wiping her mouth carefully with a napkin, then propping her elbows on the table and leaning toward him.

"This little town has good pizza. And delicious Greek pastries."

This was how their talks often started—one of them would drop a bomb and wait for the other to react. One reason he was a good attorney was that he'd learned long ago how *not* to show his emotions, thanks to Sylvie. But he swallowed hard now, struggling to maintain his neutral expression. He finally gave it up.

"You met Jade? How is she?"

The last question came out in a rush, sounding desperate. He shouldn't care. But he had to know.

"Ticked off," Sylvie replied. "Upset. Hurt. Gathering her friends around her for support." One corner of her mouth lifted. "You may find yourself getting a cool reception from the local townsfolk."

No surprise there. But he was glad to know Jade had friends like that. Better friends than him. Sylvie rested her chin in one hand, tapping her cheek thoughtfully with her finger as she stared straight at him.

"I like her. She's smart. She's tough. She's not going to take any BS, not even from you. Not even when she's in love with you." She paused. "Oh, and by the way—you're a complete idiot. Like...world-class level of stupid to dump that woman. And so slimy to do it when she's eight months pregnant. Who *are* you right now?"

"I didn't *dump* her. I just told her I think it's best if we stay friends instead of...anything more than that." He sat back and folded his arms on his chest. "Why are you *here*, Sylvie?"

"I had a feeling you were about to do something dumb." She straightened. "I could hear the *I'm not worthy* tone creeping into your voice when we talked the other day. I swear, you defeat yourself more than anyone else does. It's time to grow up, Trent."

Anger pulsed under his skin. "I'm supposed to take relationship advice from you? When you and Craig have split up and gotten back together more times than I can count?"

Her eyes narrowed. "At least we didn't give up."

"I didn't *give up* with Cindy. She left me, remember?"

"How could I forget when you wear the wound like a yoke that's been chained on your back for the rest of time? And as far as Craig and I go, we've done the work to get past our demons. You should be *happy* for us, you jerk. He went to rehab and hasn't had a drink in over a year, and I've finally found a therapist who could untangle all *my* baggage and help me cut myself free of it. When people love each other, they do the work, Trent."

"Cindy and I loved each other, and we—"

"No you didn't." He started to argue, but she stopped him. "You may have loved her, although I've always thought you loved the idea of an instant family more than her. But she *never* loved you. She toyed with you like a cat does with a mouse. She took Harper away, knowing what it would do to you, and not caring what it did to that little girl. No one who loved you would do that. You don't want to hear it, but she played you from the start, brother."

He worked his jaw back and forth, knowing she wasn't wrong. Her voice softened.

"Was it the news about Dad that made you blow things up with Jade? Or the news about Cindy sending Harper to live a nice, normal life with her grandparents? And why the hell didn't you tell Jade about Harper?"

He looked up. "You *told* her?"

For the first time since she'd breezed into his suite, she looked uncomfortable. "I had no idea you were keeping all these secrets. Which, by the way, is a horrible way to start a relationship. I told Jade it was your story to tell." Her voice grew firmer. "And you need to go to her and tell it." She reached over and took his hand in hers. "Don't let one mistake scare you away from being with Jade."

"One?" He barked out a laugh. "You think I've only made one mistake?" He shook his head sharply, pulling his hand from hers. "Didn't you tell me the last time you left Craig that our family was cursed when it came to relationships? Dad is ending marriage number *four*. Mom's on her second. You've broken up and reunited three times so far. We have no road map to follow for successful relationships, Sylvie. We've never even *seen* one!" His voice had risen to a near shout. He took a breath and held it a moment to settle himself.

"Trent…" Sylvie's voice was low and soft. "You can't let fear rule your life."

"It's not fear." The words felt hollow when he said them. "It's… lessons learned. It's…it's…" *Was* it fear? He shook his head again.

"Are you willing to lose Jade over whatever it is that you're calling it?" Sylvie stood and reached for her jacket. "I only spent half an hour with the woman, but I have a feeling she is perfectly capable of running a business and raising a baby on her own. So think about what you're willing to lose, little brother." She headed for the door, but turned as she took the handle, staring back to where he was still sitting, frozen in place. "That's what brought Craig and I back together—neither of us was willing to give up."

"And if you break up again?"

"Then we'll keep *trying*! That's the difference between Craig and I and you and Cindy. Craig and I love each other. We never *stopped* loving each other, even when things were a mess. Even when we had to be apart. But you and Cindy were dysfunctional from the get-go." Her head tipped to the side. "Do you miss her?"

"Cindy? Hell, no!"

"Do you miss Jade?"

With every heartbeat...

"It's only been a day."

"Okay, *will* you miss her if she gives up on you and moves on?"

He had a vision of an enormous chasm opening before him, dark and empty. His life without Jade in it. Sylvie chuckled as she opened the door.

"That's what I thought. Let's have breakfast in the morning. I don't head home until tomorrow night."

He sat at the table until the room grew dark around him.

Do you miss Jade?

Yes, it had only been a day. And yes, he missed

her so much his whole being ached with it. But he'd done it for *her*. He'd meant what he said to his sister—he had no idea how to navigate a successful relationship. Add a child to the mix, and things got even murkier.

The wound was new and raw and painful. It would heal as time went by, though. Jade would come to see that getting mixed up with him long-term, other than as a co-parent, was a bad idea. That *loving* him was a bad idea.

Think about what you're willing to lose...

He couldn't shake the feeling that he may have just made a terrible mistake.

"Joe, have I told you lately how much I love you?" Jade watched as Joe slid a tray of festive Christmas cookies into the display case. "You have single-handedly saved the day. Thank you."

As usual, he seemed uncomfortable with the compliment, and just gave a nod in response. She knew he had a hard time with praise, but she couldn't help herself. Anyone looking at the quiet guy, slightly built and silver-haired, would think he was a mechanic or an electrician or something technical and blue-collar. They would never say *artist*, but that's exactly what he was. And he made it seem effortless.

When he'd first come to work for her, she'd had so many reservations. His age, for one. But she'd been pleasantly surprised to learn that even though he told her he'd "retired" from the grocery store bakery, he was only in his late fifties. He'd been working in the grocery store to supplement his military retirement, and had simply grown bored of just baking bread day after day. He wanted to do something more creative.

She'd been concerned Joe might not be able to tackle the Greek pastry recipes, with their delicate flavors and tender phyllo crusts. But he'd quickly picked up on everything, and had brought new skills, like the hand-painted Christmas cookies he'd just finished. Angels, ornaments, children, puppies—each one was colorful and unique. Today was the first day he'd tackled all the baking on his own, with help from Pat. It had been a trial run for when Jade started her maternity leave, and everything had gone smoothly.

In the few months since the shop opened, the place had found its niche and was doing steady, and profitable, business. She reminded herself for the third or fourth time that morning that she should grab a bottle of water to drink. She'd been out of sorts all week and skipped her usual routine of drinking a big glass as soon as she got out of bed.

The bakery had settled into a routine of daily specials that local customers had already memorized—kunafa nests on Wednesdays and Saturdays, baklava and bougatsa on Tuesdays and Fridays. It was all coming together.

If only her personal life would.

A few days ago, she'd thought she was close to perfection in that department. In love with a wonderful man. About to have a daughter together. Planning a future. For once in her life, she'd felt like she *belonged.* She couldn't have been more wrong.

She hadn't seen Trent since Monday night, when he'd announced he was ending their relationship. That he was doing her a *favor.* Gee, what a guy. Now it was Friday. Jade wiped down the tea counter. It was already spotless, but she needed *something* to do. She looked out the window at the falling snowflakes and sighed.

Sylvie had stopped by briefly before heading home to Colorado. She hadn't said much about Trent, other than he was being a fool, but he had his reasons. That might be true, but if he couldn't talk to Jade about them, then his *reasons* weren't the issue. His refusal to *deal* with them was. She needed a partner she could rely on, and until he sorted out his feelings, Trent wasn't it.

She wiped down the tabletops, then took a seat. She'd been so tired all week, with hardly any real sleep. She'd forgotten to get a bottle of water before she sat, but she'd grab one when she went in the kitchen. She did her best to convince herself that she was doing the right thing. That she was being logical. That she was embracing self-care by knowing her boundaries and setting limits. Her therapist would be so proud.

So why was her heart breaking? Why couldn't she sleep at night? Why did she sometimes think she should go knock on the door to Trent's suite and beg him to reconsider? Her hand clenched the cleaning cloth so tightly that a puddle of water formed on the table. She wiped it up, scolding herself. If she had to beg Trent to love her, then he'd clearly never loved her in the first place. At least, he hadn't loved her enough.

The bell tinkled above the door, and she looked up to greet the customer. Pat was at the counter, giving her a warning look as if to say *this is my job*. It was Dan Adams, in uniform under his waist-length winter jacket. Here for his near-daily visit for something sweet to share with his wife, Mack, over lunch.

"Hi, Dan!" Jade smiled. "Is it lunchtime already?"

"I'm a little early. I've got a court case this afternoon, so Mack suggested we do brunch instead. She made a quiche, and I'm bringing the sweets, as usual. Is today a bougatsa day?"

"You know it is—you know my menu better than I do." She went to stand, but Dan motioned for her to stay seated. Pat was already putting a large square of the cream-filled pastry into a bag for him. It was interesting how conflicted she felt—glad Joe and Pat could run the business, and feeling a bit obsolete as she watched them do it.

Dan stopped by the table after he'd cashed out, looking down at her with concern in his eyes. "How are you doing?"

"Great!" She made her voice as perky as possible. "Joe and Pat have the shop under control. Bunny's got another month in the oven." She patted the tight, round beachball at her waist, and got a quick kick in response. "Basically, I'm just hanging out in waiting mode."

"And Bunny's daddy? How's he doing?"

Her smile trembled for a second, and she bit her lower lip to control it. "No idea."

"He's still being a jerk, huh?" Dan shook his head. "We men are not the brightest bulbs in the box sometimes. Don't give up on him. He'll pull his head out his butt eventually. I did."

She nodded with a polite smile. She'd heard plenty of stories over the past four days about how her friends' marriages almost didn't happen, but then miraculously things worked out. It was sweet, and there might even be grains of truth to the stories, but Jade had never been one to believe in miracles. She believed in things she could see. Bunny shifted inside her, giving her a firm kick to the diaphragm. *Or* things she could tangibly feel.

Life wasn't sunshine and roses just because you wanted it to be. She glanced out the window at the snow, which was growing heavier and beginning to cover the road, turning the world into a monochrome photograph. Black and white. Just like life.

You win or you lose. People love you or they don't.

They stay with you or they leave. Wishing wouldn't change that. Neither would waiting.

"I appreciate it, Dan. Gallant Lake seems to be full of happily-ever-afters, but sometimes things just don't work out. I think it's better if I accept it and move on."

He started to speak, stopped as if changing his mind, then pushed ahead again. "That sounds very... practical...of you. But love isn't always—"

She shook her head sharply. "I don't know of any magic potion that will *make* someone love me. And I'm sure as hell not going to beg for it."

"That's fair. But are you willing to give up the *chance* of a little magic happening? That whatever Trent is doing or feeling might be a speed bump and not a dead end?" He reached for the door. "Are you willing to lose him?"

The ringing wall phone saved her from coming up with an answer to three very good questions. Pat was in back helping Joe, so Jade got up to catch the call. As soon as it rang the third time, it would roll over to voicemail, but she prided herself on having the small-town personal touch and answering the phone.

She'd only taken two steps when she heard the warning roar in her ears. *Oh no.* Not here. Not in front of Dan. She said a silent promise to drink more water as soon as she took care of the phone call.

Just let me get behind the counter to the chair. I'll be fine.

Dark shadows narrowed her vision. But she could still see the phone. And the chair. They were so far away.

Just a few more steps—I can do this.

I can...

Someone yelled her name.

Glass shattered.

Darkness.

Chapter Sixteen

Trent was tossing his leather satchel in the back of his SUV when his phone rang. He was on his way to a meeting in Hunter with Vince Grassman and the president of the Save Our New York Mountains organization. SONYM was a newer lobbying group, but they'd grown quickly with the recent threats of fracking and increased interest in logging and mining in both the Catskills and the larger Adirondacks. Vince said they needed a good environmental attorney on staff.

He pulled out his phone as he slid behind the wheel. Mackenzie Adams from the liquor store. He let it go to voicemail, figuring she was just another of Jade's circle of friends wanting to talk about the magic of love and telling yet another story of overcoming hardship to find The One. This town had a thing about romance. They couldn't seem to understand the concept of loving someone so much you needed to *protect* them. That's what he was doing with Jade. Protecting her.

His mouth went sour. After four days without her, even *he* was having a hard time believing his own excuses. His sister's words kept bouncing around his brain. *What are you willing to lose?* And her parting words when he drove her to JFK. *Stop being such a coward.*

He sat there with the engine running, but still in park. Who was he kidding? He couldn't fathom a world where he saw Jade constantly because of their daughter, but where he had to resist loving her. Where he had to pretend instead of taking the risk.

His grip tightened on the steering wheel. Sylvie was right—he was an idiot. He was finally building the life he'd dreamed of…and now he was excluding the opportunity to love someone. To be loved. Happiness had been right there at the tip of his fingers, and he'd rejected it.

Jade had never been Cindy, and never would be. What he and Jade had together was special. Precious. And he could not lose her. He refused to lose her.

He headed out of the parking lot and turned away from Gallant Lake. He'd been going out of his way to avoid driving past the bakery. Or Jade's apartment. Or anything that reminded him of her. Which was a fool's mission, because every breath he took reminded him of her.

As soon as he was finished with this interview, he was going to find Jade and tell her that. He'd tell her that of *course* he loved her. That he needed her more than the air he breathed. That he wanted a forever life with her and their daughter, and maybe more babies down the road. He'd get on his knees and beg if he had to.

The SUV's glitchy electronic system finally connected with his phone, alerting him to a new voicemail before the little blue circle started spinning again, losing signal. He was surprised Mack left a message. Usually their friends kept trying until they reached him directly to share another magical love story from this magical place. Yes, he knew that Blake and Amanda had almost given up on each other. Yes, he knew that Cassie dumped Nick when he wouldn't stop trying to protect her from the world. Yes, he knew Nate Thomas and Brittany had almost broken up when Nate thought she was lying to him about why she'd come to Gallant Lake. He chuckled to himself. Pretty soon he'd know the story behind every damn marriage in town.

The circle stopped spinning on the screen, and the message came over the speakers.

"Trent!" Mack's voice was urgent—so much so that he immediately sat up in his seat. "Jade fell at the bakery…into the display case." Trent was already pulling onto the shoulder to turn around, sending stones flying. "She passed out… Dan's there…they called the ambulance. The glass broke and Dan said she's bleeding. If you get this, please call me right away."

No need to call. He was in Gallant Lake in minutes. His tires screeched as he parked in front of the gazebo, sprinting across the street to the bakery. There was an ambulance right outside the entrance, but it was empty. His legs nearly gave way when he reached for the door and looked inside the shop. There was shattered glass all around the display case. And blood on the floor. A lot of blood…or maybe not a lot, but…more blood than he ever wanted to see.

"Jade!" He bellowed her name and ran inside.

There was a huddle of people in the corner, including two paramedics—a man and a woman. The man glanced his way while the woman stayed focused on Jade, who was sitting in a chair answering questions. That was a good sign. She didn't look up when he barged in like the Kool-Aid Man…*not* a good sign. But right now, all he cared about was that she seemed okay. There was a bandage around her forearm, and the paramedic was applying another to her scalp line above her forehead.

Dan had been kneeling at her side, but now he hurried over to Trent. "She'll be okay." Dan glanced at his watch. "You almost beat the ambulance here. Do I want to know how fast you were driving?"

"I was already in my car, and no—you don't. What happened?"

Dan shifted into police chief mode. "She got up from the table, took three wobbly steps and just… went down. Passed out cold. Took out the front of the display. She cut her right arm pretty bad— definitely needs stitches. And she might need a couple on that cut on her forehead. I think she got that one from the broken glass on the floor when she landed." He blew out a breath. "She scared the hell outta me, but I'm glad I was here."

"Me, too." Trent felt a stab of guilt. *He* should have been there. "And the baby?"

The female paramedic—her shirt said *Emily*— looked up. "You the father?"

Jade was staring at him, too. Her face was pale and tight. He could see the fear and confusion in her eyes. He took a step—he needed to hold her. But Emily shook her head. "Give us room. We'll be taking her out in a second. We just wanted to get fluids started and make sure she was stable. You riding with us?"

"Yes."

Jade barked out a laugh. "The hell you are. You don't want to be involved, remember?"

She was healthy enough to still be good and angry. That was his Jadie.

"I *never actually* said that and this isn't the time

for this conversation. I'm coming with you." He didn't want her out of his sight.

Emily held up her hand as her partner moved Jade onto the gurney and adjusted the back so she was sitting up.

"*I'm* the person who decides who rides in that rig, and if *she* doesn't want you there, you're out of luck." Emily looked back to her partner, who was frowning and speaking softly with Jade. "What's up, Miles?"

"We've got some spotting—just noticed when she moved. Not a lot, but we should get going."

Trent froze. Spotting? That meant...*bleeding*. Something wrong with the baby? Why did he feel like this was *all* his fault? They started to wheel her outside, where a small crowd of onlookers was gathering on the sidewalk. Dan put his hand on Trent's shoulder.

"Breathe, man. I don't need you passing out, too." His voice was low, for Trent only. "Right now she needs someone to be her rock."

His whole body was as tight as an overwound spring. Ready to snap. Shaking from adrenaline. He took a deep breath and nodded at Dan.

"I've got this."

He caught up with Jade behind the ambulance. Emily was firing off questions.

"Do you have abdominal pain? Have you ever spotted before? Have you felt any movement from the baby since you fell?"

It was the last question that sent Jade's hand snaking out, grabbing for his. He stepped close and took it, doing his best to look unconcerned and confident, even though his heart felt like it was going to pound right out of his chest.

"I'm here, Jade. It's going to be okay."

She searched his face and seemed to find comfort there. He was finally doing something right, after a week of doing everything wrong.

"Come with me." She squeezed his hand more tightly.

"Wild horses couldn't keep me away."

They lifted her into the ambulance and he scrambled in and took the little jump seat next to her, opposite where Emily was working. Miles climbed into the front to drive. Dan swung the doors shut, giving Trent one last reassuring look.

"I'll help Joe and Pat get things cleaned up here."

Emily was trying to find a pulse for the baby, but she explained they shouldn't panic if she didn't. She didn't have a fetal heart monitor in the truck. Miles called out that they were heading for the hospital in Monticello, which would take fifteen or twenty minutes.

Trent scowled. "There isn't a hospital closer than that?" Emily saw the tension on his face and gave him a quick smile, apparently deciding he wasn't the enemy.

"It's the Catskills, Dad. There isn't a hospital on

every mountain. Better we get there in one piece than try to break any speed records." She sat back, giving up on finding a pulse. "You're eight months, right?" Jade nodded.

Emily patted Jade's free hand, which was resting on Bunny. "You landed on your side, and a mother's body does a wonderful job of protecting babies in the womb. Your little one is floating around in all that water, and it's like being cushioned in bubble wrap. They can take quite a fall with their mommies and be just fine."

"Then why isn't she moving?"

"Does she usually move 24/7?"

Jade shook her head, and Emily nodded with a smile.

"I didn't think so. You probably scared the day-lights out of her. If *you* relax, *she'll* relax." She glanced at Jade's tight grip on Trent's hand. "And if you don't unclench that hand a little, you're going to bleed through your bandage, not to mention break your husband's hand. Take a deep breath, hold it for a second, then let it out nice and slow…that's it. And again." She looked at the monitor. "See? Your pulse is already slowing down. Keep breathing like that. Let your baby know Mom's not afraid."

Jade did as she was told, but she couldn't resist clarifying, "I don't have a husband."

Trent reached over to brush her hair from her face. "I'm your *future* husband."

She rolled her eyes. "Not gonna happen." The angry edge was fading from her voice, though. This protest was weaker than before. She met his gaze. "You left me, remember?" The ambulance had a rocking motion as it raced down the road. Looked like they were going to have this conversation here, whether he wanted to or not.

"I didn't leave you. I... I put us on hold." Her eyes narrowed and he relented. "Okay, I screwed up. It was a big, big mistake that I regret with every fiber of my being."

Jade looked over at Emily, who was clearly being entertained by the conversation. Jade gave the woman a slanted grin. "He told me he wanted to be *friends*."

"Ouch." The paramedic laughed. She looked at the monitor stats, and made a subtle nod at them for Trent's benefit. Jade's pulse was closer to normal now, and Emily clearly wanted it to stay that way. "I hope you told him to get lost."

If raking him over the coals was stabilizing her stats, he'd gladly fling himself into the flames.

Jade laughed. "I did, actually." She turned to Trent. "Wait—I told you we were done. Why are you even here?"

"I'm here..." He lifted her hand and kissed her knuckles. "Because I love you."

Her right eyebrow arched high, but there was a

softness to her gaze that warmed him. Her mouth twitched. Was she trying to hide a smile?

"That's not what you said on Monday."

"True, but that was *Monday* Trent. *Friday* Trent is a lot smarter than that other guy." He grew serious. "Monday Trent was a fool. You were right to tell *him* to take a hike. But Friday Trent...*this* Trent—" he kissed her hand again "—loves you with every fiber in his being. In fact, my actual being could vanish, and I would *still* love you."

"I have no idea what that means." Her voice was soft now, the edge gone.

"It means I'm yours if you'll have me, and I *really* want you to have me. Take me, use me, abuse me, love me...whatever. I'm yours forever, babe."

Before she could answer, Miles called out from the cab of the ambulance. "ETA five minutes!"

Jade's almost-smile faded, her lips parting in worry. "And how do I know *Monday* Trent won't show up again? How do I know you're not going to bail on me down the road?"

He thought for a moment, hating that he'd made her doubt him. "I can't tell you I won't make mistakes. That I won't overreact once in a while. My trust issues are *very* deeply rooted, Jade. But I will *never* bail on you again. You're stuck with me, Malone. For better or worse."

"You didn't tell me about your stepdaughter.

Never even mentioned her. What else haven't you told me?"

"Damn, Jade," he answered, grimacing at her directness, and admiring it at the same time. She was stronger than he was in so many ways. "Listen, I'll answer every single question you have, from now until…*forever.* Even the stuff I don't *like* to talk about. I'll lay it all on the table. I'm an open book. I'll tell you about Harper. About her mom. About my relationship with my dad. I'll tell you about my job…" He closed his eyes as he realized he hadn't contacted Vince. He glanced at his watch.

This had all happened so quickly that he wasn't even late for the meeting yet. He'd miss it, of course, but Vince would understand. And if the folks from the lobbying group didn't understand, then it wasn't the right job for him anyway.

"What job?" Jade asked.

"The one I was hoping to land this afternoon." He shrugged, talking over her when she started to apologize. "It's okay. I'll call from the hospital and reschedule. Right now I'm where I need to be."

"You were taking a job here in New York? Even after we…?"

"In the deepest reaches of Monday Trent's brain, even *he* knew there was no way he'd leave you. No way he didn't love you." He swallowed hard. "I'm so sorry I hurt you, baby. I'll spend the rest of my life making it up to you."

The ambulance was slowing, going through a bit more traffic, turning at intersections, sending them all rocking in the back. Jade's eyes went wide, her free hand flattening on her stomach. Her smile was bright.

"It's Bunny!"

Emily leaned forward in concern. "*What's* bunny?"

"Bunny is a *who*," Trent explained, sagging with relief. "We call the baby *Bunny*. She moved?"

Jade nodded, her eyes closing as her head fell back against the gurney. "I just felt her. Oh…" She giggled. "…There she is again!"

"No pain?" Emily asked.

"None at all." Jade looked into Trent's eyes, as the ambulance backed toward the emergency entrance at the hospital. "Not any more."

The ambulance doors flew open, and Emily snapped back to business, detailing to the attendants what had happened and what the current situation was. He jumped out with Jade and the orderly looked at him.

"Family?" he demanded.

Jade answered before he could.

"Yes." She gave his hand a little squeeze. "He's family."

Jade slid into the back seat of Blake Randall's limo with a loud sigh of relief. It was eight o'clock at night, and she was exhausted.

The doctors had insisted that she stick around the ER for a while after she got her stitches—thirty in her arm and five on her forehead. The OB/GYN consult wanted to be sure everything was fine with Bunny, as well as keeping an eye on Jade's blood pressure. The spotting had stopped, and the doctor said it was probably a minor placental abruption. There was no fluid with it, and the amount of blood was minimal. Enough to be scary to *Jade*, but not to the doctors. They blamed her fainting on allowing herself to become dehydrated again, as well as being overtired.

Trent closed the door behind her and went to the other side of the limo, where the driver, Stewart, was holding the door for him. He came inside and slid over to put his arms around her shoulders. She happily leaned into his embrace, resting her head on his shoulder. He loved her. She let out a happy sigh.

"This is the way to travel, right?" She looked around as Stewart pulled out of the hospital parking lot. "I can't believe Blake and Amanda sent an actual limo for us. I'm surprised Amanda wasn't hiding inside. Or one of the other Gallant Lake ladies, ready to talk some more about their love stories." They'd all texted at least once since her unexpected ambulance ride a few hours ago.

Trent kissed the top of her head, and she felt him shaking with laughter.

"They did that to *you*, too?" he asked. "I think I

know the backstory to every wedding in town. I was waiting for one of the guys to try to sell me some Gallant Lake Love Potion or something." He pulled her closer. "And the only reason they *weren't* all piled into the limo ready to pounce was because I made Blake promise we'd have this ride all to ourselves."

"Not that I don't love them, but…thank you." She closed her eyes. "I can't wait to get home and sleep in my own bed."

"Uh…"

She lifted her head. "What?"

"Two things, actually. The doctor said I need to wake you every hour or so to make sure you don't have a concussion." He kissed her forehead again. "I'll make it as quick as possible, but it's gotta be done. And…we're not going back to your place. We're going to my suite."

She pushed away from him. She wasn't so tired that she couldn't give him a piece of her mind about being ordered around. But he took her hands in his and clasped them together, staring straight into her eyes.

"I'm not trying to be Bossy McBoss Man here. But this is nonnegotiable. You passed out into a plate-glass display case today, Jade."

She winced at the residual fear still haunting his expression. For something so dramatic, she didn't remember one bit of it. One minute she was walking to the counter, and the next thing she knew, Dan was calling her name from above her and she was trying to figure out why she was on the floor. And where all that blood was coming from. Trent tugged her hands gently, and she relented, sliding back into his arms as he continued.

"Your place has way too many long, metal staircases. I didn't like those things before, and I *really* don't like them now. Too dangerous."

"That may be, but I can't live in your hotel room."

"You can for now. Brittany's reaching out to the owners of that house by the ski lodge we liked. If that doesn't work out, we'll find something else."

He'd obviously been busy on his phone at the hospital while she'd been resting. Which reminded her...

"Were you able to reschedule the job interview?"

"Yup. Tuesday morning." He rested his head on hers. "And we're meeting in Gallant Lake, so I don't have to leave you for long."

"I don't need a babysitter, Trent." She was so used to taking care of herself that, even pregnant and injured, she didn't want to give up her independence. At the same time, she felt an unfamiliar surge of love and security. She had someone who cared enough to take charge when needed.

"I don't want you to feel like I'm babysitting you, but you're going to have to accept me being a little overprotective for a while."

"Oh I will, huh?" For some reason, the idea of Trent taking care of her didn't seem bad at all. "Well,

I guess it will give us lots of time to explore that *open book* you promised me."

He stilled, then nodded against her. "Whatever you want to know. And a few things you probably *don't* want to know, but you'll get it anyway."

She closed her eyes. She'd never forget the sight of Trent bursting into the bakery, yelling her name like he thought she was dead. The panic in his eyes… She frowned. He'd left her out of fear. Was he coming *back* out of fear, too?

Or was it guilt? When the doctor in the ER explained that she'd probably fainted because she was dehydrated and hadn't been sleeping well, Trent had taken that personally. He'd said it was *his* fault. Which…was kinda true. At least, he'd instigated the stress that made her careless, but the carelessness was on her.

Jade sat up again, looking into his whiskey eyes so she could gauge his honesty. "Why are you really doing this? Are we back on again because of my accident? Did I *scare* you into coming back? Because I am not going to fling myself into plate glass every time you try to leave me."

He started to laugh, then saw she wasn't kidding.

"Babe, I'd already realized what a fool I'd been. I knew I couldn't live without you."

"But what *made* you realize that? Is it just because I got hurt?"

"What? No!" He stopped. "I was going to find

you after my interview—I was going to tell you everything. The fall just…accelerated it a little. I've never felt fear like that, and don't ever want to again."

"I can't help thinking you're only back because I fell. It was an ambulance confession of love." The man with trust issues had given her a few of her own.

Trent turned in his seat, cupping her face in his hands, coming so close their noses nearly touched. "I don't have an email to show you to prove what my plans were, but *please*, babe. I have never lied to you. Yes, I didn't tell you some things, but I never lied." He paused. "Except when I denied loving you. When I saw the ambulance…when I thought of losing you. If anything had happened with you still thinking I *didn't* love you? I'd never be able to live with myself." He rested his forehead against hers, his words moving across her skin with his breath. "When Sylvie was here, she asked me what I was willing to lose if I refused to let myself love again. And Jade, I am *not* willing to lose you. I am *not* willing to lose our daughter. We are a…" He grinned. "What did *Monday* Trent call it? A family unit. It's what we'll *always* be. Just give me the chance to prove it, babe. Give *us* a chance."

She wanted to be careful. To protect her heart. To protect Bunny. But as hard as she tried, she couldn't convince herself that Trent was a risk. He'd stumbled. He'd panicked. He was human. But he loved her. And for once in her life, she belonged some-where. She belonged with him.

She tipped her head so she could press her lips to his, earning a soft moan from him. The kiss was tender. Soft. Yet so full of truth and love that Jade didn't want it to end. But the limo had come to a stop in front of the Gallant Lake Resort. Trent pulled back, leaving a playful kiss on the tip of her nose as he did.

"Maybe all of our friends were right about Gallant Lake having a bit of magic."

She giggled. "Well, Amanda swears their house is haunted by a romance-loving spirit from the past. Maybe Madeleine the Ghost leaves Halcyon once in a while to sprinkle love dust around."

"I think Madeleine finally caught up with us."

Chapter Seventeen

They spent the next few days dividing their time between house hunting and talking. *Lots* of talking. Jade realized how much Trent had been letting his insecurities weigh him down, sending him into that panic spiral. The more he talked, no matter how painful the topic, the more she could see his tensions easing. And as he relaxed, so did she—the last of her doubts evaporating.

She'd reluctantly agreed not to work that weekend. It's not like she could do much anyway with her right arm wrapped from her elbow to her fingers. And Joe and Pat were going to have to handle the bakery on their own in another month or so anyway. They'd cleared all the broken glass and cleaned up. For now the counter was an open display until the replacement glass—*safety* glass this time—arrived in a few weeks.

Trent shared what it was like to grow up with two parents locked in some sort of vengeful competition, with Trent and Sylvie in the middle. After their divorce, both parents had gone through relationships like water. His mother was happily married now, but she'd dated a long line of "uncles" when Trent was a teen, and his father was constantly bringing different women home. There were always strangers moving in and out of his life. Some were nice, some ignored him, and some had no problem telling him they wanted him out of their hair.

He talked about his father and his conditional love through the years. As far as Alfred Michaels was concerned, only *winners* mattered. He expected his children, and especially his son, to be the best at everything—top of his class, dean's list, best job, biggest house, nicest car. It wasn't how hard you *tried*. To him, effort meant nothing if you didn't come out on top. And while *he'd* married and divorced multiple times, he treated Trent like a failure for not being able to make *his* marriage work.

With all of that, Trent still loved his father and craved his approval. That was why he'd continually tried to find that *one thing* that might satisfy the man. He'd been in and out of therapy through the years, and even his therapist had told him to stop trying to do the impossible. Trent said it wasn't until

he fell in love with Jade that he realized it was time
to let it all go. He couldn't *change* his father, but
he could change how he reacted to him. And if his
father couldn't handle that, it wasn't on Trent. And
he finally told Jade everything about his marriage
to Cindy. He and Jade had been in bed after sunset
on Saturday, tangled up in bedsheets and each other.
With his head on her chest and his arms wrapped
around her—one hand resting on Bunny—he told
her that Cindy had swept into his life at a holiday
office party.

"She was there as someone else's date," he said
with a low laugh. "That should have told me something."

He said she was clever and pretty and full of energy. She enjoyed hiking and camping, or so she
said when they were dating. Once they were married, everything was a different story. But there was
a child involved—*her* child, Harper, who was four
when they met. Trent said he'd tried to adopt her, but
Cindy was constantly changing her mind about it.

"In her defense," he said, "I think she had some
issues that left her…unstable. She'd be upbeat and
laughing one day, then in a white-hot rage the next.
And when she was in a rage…" He sighed. "It was
pretty obvious she was cheating on me—after a
while, she didn't even bother to hide it. She told me
I was boring, but I think she was more disappointed
that I wasn't quite as wealthy as she'd thought. I

stayed as long as I did more for Harper than for Cindy. She was a great kid, and I wanted her to have some stability."

By the time Trent finished telling Jade the story, including the day he came home to no furniture *and* no family in the house, she understood why he'd never wanted to talk about it. She ran her fingers through his hair, feeling his sorrow over the failed marriage, and his frustration at losing contact with Harper without ever having a chance to say *goodbye*.

"Your sister was right. Cindy was abusive to you," Jade said softly.

He lifted his head. "No. No, she didn't hit me or anything like that." He gave her a slanted, humorless smile. "She broke a few vases, but never over my head."

"A person doesn't need to get physical to be abusive." She lifted her head and gave him a soft kiss on the lips. "She was erratic, she lied, she cheated…" She bit back the hurt and anger she felt on his behalf. "Even if there were legitimate mental reasons behind it, the effect was still the same to you. And then she left you in a way she knew would hurt you the most—by taking Harper away without warning."

Trent shifted so that his face was close to hers. "I tried to convince her to let me see Harper after she left, if only to explain things and say goodbye, but she insisted a 'clean break' was best. I didn't have any parental rights, so I just…had to live with it."

"I'm so sorry, baby." Her fingers kept tracing through his hair. "Knowing all of this makes everything that's happened with us make so much more sense." His inability to trust—not only not trusting others, but not trusting his own judgment. His fear of losing Bunny. "It must have been hard to carry all of this around inside of you."

"Maybe I shouldn't have stopped seeing my therapist, but I thought I had it under control. It messed with my head. And worse, it messed with *us*." He ran his fingers across her cheek with a grin. "And now I've dumped it all on you."

"You *shared* it with me." She corrected him. "Now we carry it together. Or even better? We let it all go and start our lives over with a clean slate."

He considered that, and his smile deepened. "Easier said than done, but we're stronger together than apart." He shifted around so he was looking down into her face. "I may not believe in a lot of things, but God knows, I believe in you and me."

She wrapped her arms around his neck with a sigh, her heart full and satisfied. "I'm glad to hear it, Whiskey, because I'm not going anywhere."

Chapter Eighteen

Trent let out a loud groan when the mattress shifted before dawn. It was their third night in the rental house, and he'd really been hoping for a few consecutive hours of sleep.

"Sorry," Jade whispered. "I swear, Bunny has been elbowing my bladder ever since we moved in."

"S'okay, babe. Sleep is overrated." He put his hand in the small of her back to steady her as she rolled herself into a sitting position, then stood and headed to the bathroom.

She called out to him from the master bath. "Don't let me forget to look for a night-light to put in here if we're out today."

"Um…it's the day before Christmas. I don't think we want to be anywhere near a store today."

"We have to go into town so I can pick up the bread Joe promised to bake for me. That's my contribution to Christmas dinner at the Randalls'. That and dessert, of course, but I'll make the bougatsa here this afternoon."

She walked back to the bed, her soft cotton nightgown draping over her swollen belly. She slid into bed and he opened his arms to welcome her. She snuggled next to him, her head on his shoulder.

"Maybe you could run over to the hardware store and see if Nate has any?"

Trent frowned. "Any *what*?"

"Uh…night-lights?"

"Oh…yeah, sure. I've got a list of things we need from him." He kissed her hair. "Meanwhile, it's five a.m. Let's get a little more sleep before we add more things to our to-do lists."

"What did you think about what Asher said about updating the house?" She paused. "Sorry, I'm wide awake."

He chuckled, pulling the blankets higher to cover her shoulders. "Which means *I'm* wide awake, apparently."

Asher and Nora had been two of their many helpers on moving day. Asher, an architect, had spent a lot of time walking around the house with Trent. They were renting for now, but the owner was hoping to sell it. The house was straight out of the seventies—complete with harvest-gold appliances and shag carpeting in the basement rec room.

But it was a big house on a gently sloping two-acre lot below the ski lodge on Watcher Mountain. A short drive to town—and the bakery—with great views of Gallant Lake this time of year. When the trees below them leafed out in the summer, some of that view would be hidden, but the property itself had been beautifully landscaped at one time. It just needed some TLC.

"So you agree we should buy the place?" He turned on his side and brushed her hair from her face. "We don't have to rush, you know. We barely have enough furniture at this point." And what they had was a mash-up of stuff that had been in storage from their respective apartments.

"I know." Jade sighed. "But it already feels like home to me. Maybe it's my maternal nesting instincts kicking in."

"We'll start padding the nest next week, mama bird. I'll start painting and you and your girlfriends can go shopping for nursery furniture…and maybe a nice sofa for the living room while you're at it. And a really big TV." He kissed her soft and welcoming lips. "Once this baby girl arrives…" He stroked her taut belly. "…Then we'll think about whether this is our forever home."

They lay together in silence. He was at peace. It wasn't a familiar feeling, but it was a nice one. He felt *totally* at peace. Content. Secure in Jade's love at last. And about to be a father.

She snuggled closer. "Have you thought about a name?"

"For Bunny? I thought you wanted to meet her first?"

She pursed her lips. "We should probably narrow it down to a few choices, though, don't you think? My mom's name was Daphne, but I'm not sure—"

He blew out a long sigh. "Babe, I love you more than anything, but I am not prepared for all this decision-making before dawn." His hand was still on her baby bump, and he began to massage her with his fingertips. "I tell you what…if you'll *try* to go to sleep for a few more hours, maybe Santa will give you one of your presents tonight instead of Christmas morning."

Her eyes narrowed. "Uh… Christmas Eve is when I'm *supposed* to get my presents."

"I'm with Kevin Costner in *Bull Durham* on this one. I believe in opening presents on Christmas morning, not Christmas Eve. But I'll make an exception for you." He gave her a quick kiss, his fingers still stroking her stomach. "*If* you go to sleep right now."

"Just keep doing that thing with your fingers. It feels good."

"Usually I'm doing something a little more interesting when a woman says that."

"Yeah? Well I'm guessing none of those women was about to pop out your baby, were they?"

He snorted. "Not a single one. Close your eyes and try to stop thinking so much. You need your rest as much as I do. Count sheep or something."

He massaged her stomach until her breathing slid into a slow, steady rhythm. Tonight was the night. Sylvie had sent what he'd asked for, after grilling him on what it was and why he had it and why he wanted it in Gallant Lake. And now it was in a box under the tree that Dan and Mack had put up and decorated the day he and Jade moved in. The tree was real, but since it was bought during Christmas week, it was a bit scraggly. Still, their friends had collected enough loaner decorations to decorate *ten* trees, so things were festive.

It would make a perfect backdrop for a wedding proposal.

Jade was spending Christmas Eve pregnant and in love with a great guy. She was going to have his baby...*very* soon. They'd found a funky-but-loveable house to live in. They even had a *Christmas tree*. And...there were *presents* under it. Presents for *her*. Jade loved getting presents.

There were a few gifts under the tree for Trent, too, of course. Most were things she'd ordered on-line, since she hadn't had a lot of time or energy for shopping. She'd set up a new work schedule with Joe,

Pat and two part-timers who were going to cover the bakery for the next few months.

As much as she'd wanted to keep working, her doctor had agreed with Trent that it was time to stop.

Trent had been dead serious about opening gifts Christmas morning and *not* on Christmas Eve. But he'd promised one gift tonight, and had directed her to the overstuffed armchair near the tree. He was perched on the ottoman next to her, getting far too much enjoyment from knowing she wanted to open every single brightly wrapped package. Not only was he only allowing her to open *one*, he was going to select *which* one.

She was tempted to hand him a package of hiking socks to open, saving the box of climbing gear Nick West had helped her select for Trent's precious Christmas morning. It would serve him right. Instead, she relented and handed him the box of equipment—carabiners, a harness, lanyards and a bunch of other stuff she had no idea what he was going to do with. Trent seemed thrilled—apparently Nick had known exactly what brands he preferred and what equipment he was looking for.

And now Trent was handing her a…shoebox? He'd gone *shoe* shopping? As if she needed shoes. Especially eight months pregnant. Especially considering there were other packages under the tree that were clearly the size of jewelry boxes. She managed to hide her opinion, though. They were a new couple, and he had plenty of time to learn how to properly gift in the future. She'd give him a pass for this, their first—and rushed—Christmas.

"I can't wait to see what's inside!" she said, flashing him a bright smile.

He returned the smile, but he seemed nervous. Maybe he knew shoes weren't the greatest choice for Christmas Eve. At least the wrapping was pretty. The heavy ivory paper was gilded with gold stars, with a matching satin bow. She carefully unwrapped it, sliding her fingernail under the tape to release it, sliding the box out. The brand on the box was for sneakers. Her brows rose—sneakers weren't a bad idea for the bakery. Very practical. And somewhat disappointing.

But she didn't find a pair of sneakers inside. In fact, she didn't find a *pair* of anything. There was one shoe. And it looked very familiar. Because it was *her* shoe...from the night they'd met. She pulled the shimmering slingback out of the box, confused yet delighted.

"You *kept* this? Oh, my God!" She laughed. "We should frame it, or maybe put it under glass." She held it up. "The shoe that started a family! Or at least the *mate* of the shoe that started one. The shoe you caught me murdering is out there in the lake somewhere." She laughed again. "This is the weirdest and best gift I've ever received!"

He was smiling, but there was something else in

his expression. Anticipation? Anxiety? As if there was something he was waiting for her to see or say. She glanced in the box, but there was nothing there but tissue paper. What was she missing?

Light bounced off the bejeweled shoe she was holding. *Wait.* Those shoes weren't bejeweled. There weren't any rhinestones on them. She inspected the shoe more closely. Something was dangling from the strap.

It was a ring. A *diamond* ring. A ring with *many* diamonds. She looked up, but Trent wasn't on the ottoman anymore. He was on one knee in front of her. She was too stunned to move, so he took the shoe, unbuckled the strap, dropped the ring into his hand, and slid it onto her finger with a wide smile and a sigh of relief.

"Oh, good—it fits." His eyes met hers. "Jade Malone, soon-to-be mother of my daughter and keeper of my heart forever, will you marry me?"

She stared at him, still speechless. He chuckled, reaching up with his fingers to gently lift her chin… and close her open mouth.

"I know the ring's already on your finger, but I kinda need to hear your answer, babe." He held her hand in his, turning it so the ring caught the light like a flame. "I love you, Jade. I want you to be my wife. It doesn't need to happen before Bunny arrives. If you want to wait and have the biggest wedding Gallant Lake has ever seen, that's fine with me. But marry me." His smile faded, and he actually looked nervous. "Please."

She cupped his face with her hands. She would have leaned forward, but Bunny was in the way.

"Of *course* I'll marry you, Trent Michaels." Her heart swelled with joy. A life filled with love stretched out in front of her, bright and inviting.

He rose onto his knees and kissed her, his arms sliding around her. The kiss started tender, then quickly turned heated. The only thing that separated them was a vigorous kick from their daughter. Trent laughed against her mouth, then pulled away, shaking his head in amusement.

"I hope that's a celebration kick, and not a warning."

"She's just mad that she won't be able to dance at our wedding, which will *definitely* happen before she comes into the world."

"If that's what you want, that's what we'll do." He stood and pulled her to her feet with him. "I don't know how, considering she's due on what...the twentieth?...but you know I'll make it happen."

Jade rolled her eyes. "You're cute, the way you keep forgetting I can make things happen all by myself."

His head fell back and he laughed. "You are absolutely right. Again. Our life will never be dull, will it?" He put his hand on her stomach. "Especially if this little one is half as lively as you are. The two of you are going to keep me on my toes."

As if to agree, the baby kicked again, right where his hand was.

Jade smiled. "That's the plan, Whiskey Guy."

Epilogue

"I remember standing in this very spot, waiting for *my* pregnant bride-to-be." Blake Randall nudged Trent's arm. "But she wasn't as pregnant as Jade. In fact, she and I were the only ones who knew. I can't believe you guys made it until today without having that baby."

Trent was a little surprised himself, especially after Jade had a few cramps last week. They'd rushed to the doctor's office, but he'd proclaimed it a false alarm and sent them home.

He and Blake were standing in the grand hall of Halcyon. A drape of blue hydrangeas and white roses—Greek colors for Jade—hung from the massive marble fireplace. The Randalls had offered the home, which had been the setting for more than one Gallant Lake wedding, to Trent and Jade on Christmas Day, as everyone was oohing and ahhing over the engagement ring.

"Yep." Nick West nodded at their side. "I stood here, too, but only while I was waiting. It was summertime and Cassie wanted the ceremony out on the veranda. This place has seen a lot of weddings."

More friends were standing nearby, talking softly amongst themselves and waiting for the bride to arrive.

There would be a much larger and more formal celebration in the summer where everyone from St. Louis and Denver would be invited. Both of their families were a little miffed to be left out of this one, but they also understood that there had been a very real chance of this wedding *not* happening with Jade due any minute. And everyone would want to visit after the baby was born anyway. As usual, Jade was being practical. She was also avoiding stress, per the doctor's—and Trent's—orders.

There was a flurry of activity near the library entrance, and Amanda appeared in the doorway to wave at the pianist sitting at the grand piano. He began to play, and their friends circled the fireplace, leaving an opening for Amanda and Jade. They'd decided to thank their hosts by asking them to be best man and matron of honor.

Amanda walked out first, in a simple blue sheath, carrying white roses. She patted Trent's arm with a happy grin as she took her place on the opposite side of the pastor.

Jade stepped out of the library, and everyone sighed at once. She was a vision in ivory silk, draping over her very large baby bump and trailing behind her. Mel Brannigan had managed to create a bridal gown basically out of thin air for Jade. She'd taken a dress she already had in the boutique, sliced the front of it and added a panel of silk to make it into a maternity wedding gown. It was simple. And perfect.

Jade's dark hair was swept up into a twist, secured with sparkling clips, with a lace veil hanging down her back. The baby had dropped lower since the holidays, so her walk was a bit stilted. He'd been warned not to use the word *waddle* in her vicinity, but that's exactly what she was doing. His smile faltered when he met her eyes. They were shining with excitement, and she looked happy.

But…there was a tightness in her gaze. She looked determined. Focused. And then she winced. Just barely, but enough for him to notice.

He took her hands, leaning forward to kiss her cheek and murmur, "You okay?"

She gave a quick nod. "I'm fine. Let's do this."

When they turned to the pastor, he seemed to pick up on her sense of urgency, because he moved right into the service and kept things brief. A quick prayer, a quicker message, the exchange of wedding bands with their personal vows. Halfway through hers, Jade gave a little gasp, her eyes going wide before she regrouped and continued.

And finally, Trent got it. Jade was in labor.

During. Their. Wedding. Ceremony.

As they finished and he pulled her in for a kiss, he whispered into her ear. "Am I crazy or is Bunny on the way?"

She nodded. "Big time. Let everyone take a few fast pictures and then we need to get outta here, before my water breaks."

Jade laughed as she scrolled through the wedding photos on her tablet, turning it so Trent could see.

"We should frame this one!" It was the last photo taken yesterday before she was rushed to the car and then to the hospital to deliver Arianna Daphne Michaels six hours later. Ari was now sound asleep, securely swaddled in pink in the bassinet next to Jade's hospital bed. Trent was perched on the edge of the mattress, one hand in Jade's and one hand resting with his finger touching their daughter's side. He'd hardly spent a moment where he wasn't touching, or at least gazing at, their precious little girl.

Jade never imagined she could feel so much love inside of her heart. So much that it overflowed and still just kept coming. For Trent. For Arianna. For the life they were beginning together as husband and wife. As parents. As a family. She belonged...she belonged in this life and with this man.

Trent grinned at the picture of the two of them facing each other in front of all those blue and white flowers. They were gazing into each other's eyes. It should have been a tender wedding portrait. But what the photographer captured was the moment Jade had a contraction that could *not* be hidden. The photo was snapped just as she'd let out a very loud curse word, right there in front of the pastor and their friends. Her mouth was in the shape of a perfect O. Her eyes were just as round. And Trent was mirroring her expression as he realized what was happening. His hand was a blur, reaching out to grab her arm.

"That is definitely a classic." Trent nodded. "Maybe we should put it in Ari's room, and tell her this is the moment she crashed our wedding."

Jade turned the tablet back around and gazed at the picture. "Thank God I got out of that dress before my water broke."

"The hell with the dress!" Trent laughed. "Thank God I got you out of our *car* before your water broke."

"Watch the language in front of your daughter, *Daddy*."

"Seriously? I can't even say *hell*?" He'd dropped his voice to a whisper, which made her laugh. His eyes narrowed on her. "You're busting my chops, aren't you? I was expecting more of a mellow maternal vibe from the mother of my child."

She barked out a laugh, then covered her mouth and looked to Ari, but she was still sleeping. "Have you *met* me? When have I ever given off a *mellow* vibe?"

Trent was looking at Arianna, too. "Only when you're sleeping, babe. Just like this little girl. And now I have two of you…lucky me." He moved his hand from the bassinet and turned to cup Jade's cheek. "And I *mean* that. I wouldn't have it any other way, Mrs. Michaels."

Ari began to wriggle, her little face screwing up into a pre-cry grimace. He turned back, gently lifting the eight-pound-six-ounce bundle into his hands and delivering her to Jade, who was already dropping the hospital gown from her shoulder to make her breast available.

Trent watched, his eyes filled with wonder. "I don't know who took to that faster—you or her. I mean… I know it's natural, but…it's been less than a day and you both know exactly what to do. Look at her. Look at what we did…"

Jade lowered her head to whisper to Ari, who was blissfully taking in her lunch.

"Your daddy is babbling, little girl. I think he should have taken a nap when you and Mommy did this morning." She looked over at him—her handsome, loving husband. "But he loves you so very much, just like Mommy does. You're a lucky little girl."

"You and I are the lucky ones, Jade."

She kissed the top of Ari's head, then met Trent's warm gaze.

"For a couple of people who thought they didn't do *family* well, I think we've nailed it."

He leaned forward, one hand on Arianna's tiny head and one holding Jade's shoulder. He kissed Jade's lips tenderly.

They were connected in a perfect circle of love.

* * * * *

Check out more holiday romances from
Harlequin Special Edition:

Their Texas Christmas Match
By Cathy Gillen Thacker

Starlight and the Christmas Dare
By Michelle Major

The Maverick's Christmas Secret
By Brenda Harlen

Available now wherever Harlequin Special Edition
books and ebooks are sold!

#2953 A FORTUNE'S WINDFALL
The Fortunes of Texas: Hitting the Jackpot • by Michelle Major
When Linc Maloney inherits a fortune, he throws caution to the wind and vows to live life like there's no tomorrow. His friend and former coworker Remi Reynolds thinks that Linc is out of control and tries to remind him that money can't buy happiness. She can't admit to herself that she's been feeling more than *like* for Linc for a long time but doesn't dare risk her heart on a man with a big-as-Texas fear of commitment...

#2954 HER BEST FRIEND'S BABY
Sierra's Web • by Tara Taylor Quinn
Child psychiatrist Megan Latimer would trust family attorney Daniel Tremaine with her life—but never her heart. Danny's far too attractive for any woman's good...until one night changes everything. As if crossing the line weren't cataclysmic enough, Megan and Danny just went from besties and colleagues to parents-to-be. As they work together to resolve a complex custody case, can they save a family and find their own happily-ever-after?

#2955 FALLING FOR HIS FAKE GIRLFRIEND
Sutton's Place • by Shannon Stacey
Over-the-top Molly Cyrs hardly seems a match for bookish Callan Avery. But when Molly suggests they pose as a couple to assuage Stonefield's anxiety about its new male librarian, his pretend paramour is all Callan can think about. Callan's looking for a family, though, and kids aren't in Molly's story. Unless he can convince Molly that she's not "too much"...and that to him, she's just enough!

#2956 THE BOOKSTORE'S SECRET
Home to Oak Hollow • by Makenna Lee
Aspiring pastry chef Nicole Evans is just waiting to hear about her dream job, and in the meantime, she goes to work in the café at the local bookstore. But that's before the recently widowed Nicole meets her temporary boss: her first crush, Liam Mendez! Will his simmering attraction to Nicole be just one more thing to hide...or the stuff of his bookstore's romance novels?

#2957 THEIR SWEET COASTAL REUNION
Sisters of Christmas Bay • by Kaylie Newell
When Kyla Beckett returns to Christmas Bay to help her foster mom, the last person she wants to run into is Ben Martinez. The small-town police chief just wants a second chance—to explain. But when Ben's little girl bonds with his longtime frenemy, he wonders if it might be the start of a friendship. Can the wounded single dad convince Kyla he's always wanted the best for her...then, now and forever?

#2958 A HERO AND HIS DOG
Small-Town Sweethearts • by Carrie Nichols
Former Special Forces soldier Mitch Sawicki's mission is simple: find the dog who survived the explosion that ended Mitch's military career. Vermont farmer Aurora Walsh thinks Mitch is the extra pair of hands she desperately needs. Her young daughter sees Mitch as a welcome addition to their family, whose newest member is the three-legged Sarge. Can another wounded warrior find a home with a pint-size princess and her irresistible mother?

HARLEQUIN
PLUS

Announcing a **BRAND-NEW** multimedia subscription service for romance fans like you!

Read, Watch and Play.

Experience the easiest way to get the romance content you crave.

Start your **FREE 7 DAY TRIAL** at
<u>www.harlequinplus.com/freetrial</u>.